Sex and the Single Ghost

Sex and the Single Ghost

TAWNY TAYLOR

KENSINGTON BOOKS
http://www.kensingtonbooks.com

KENSINGTON BOOKS are published by

Kensington Publishing Corp.
850 Third Avenue
New York, NY 10022

All Kensington titles, imprints and distributed lines are available at special quantity discounts for bulk purchases for sales promotion, premiums, fund-raising, educational or institutional use.

Special book excerpts or customized printings can also be created to fit specific needs. For details, write or phone the office of the Kensington Special Sales Manager: Kensington Publishing Corp., 850 Third Avenue, New York, NY 10022. Attn. Special Sales Department. Phone: 1-800-221-2647.

ISBN 0-7582-1507-X

First Kensington Trade Paperback Printing: September 2006
10 9 8 7 6 5 4 3 2 1

Printed in the United States of America

Sex and the Single Ghost

Prologue

Being dead has its advantages. Like every day is a good hair day—or bad, depending on your preference (some spirits like to be your cliché ghoul, bad hair and all). And you never have to fight rush-hour traffic on I-75 during the height of road construction season to get to the mall. Or worry about counting carbs to counteract your body's genetic predisposition to pack on the pounds after you wander through the bakery department of the grocery store.

But it has its drawbacks too. My cat, Gulliver, hates me now. I can't eat anything, including chocolate. And—this one's a biggie—I can't be touched . . . or have sex.

You see, as spirits, we can have our own form of sex. It's a silly mental-melding thing. But in my opinion it plain stinks. Without all the jittery, tingly, pitter-pattery physical parts, sex loses all its charm.

Fortunately for me, there is one night a year when we Spirit Americans (for the record, we prefer the politically correct "Spirit Americans" to the common term, "Dead") are able to have some fun. You guessed it—it's Halloween. Would any other night make sense? On our ninth, nineteenth, twenty-ninth, et cetera—you get the picture—anniversary of our passing, we are able to reanimate. In layman's terms, we gain back the body we had in physical life, minus any disease or injury associated with our passing. If during that mystical night we touch one person's heart in a positive way, we are able to remain animated for nine days and nights.

It's been nine long, tedious years since I passed and it's the eve before Halloween. I've been carefully planning my strategy and I think I have all my objectives covered. I'm going to touch one very special, hunky person's heart, and I'm going to have sex—lots of it. After all, in nine days and nine nights, I need to have enough sex to hold me over for the next ten years.

One more thing: I'm going to get some questions answered about my passing, which leads me to the hitch.

Can't forget the hitch. There's always one of those, and I bet you figured once you'd passed from this world into the next you'd finally be free of them. Sorry to disappoint you.

At exactly the stroke of midnight every night I am on earth, I must return to the place of my passing to recharge my physical battery, so to speak. Considering where I was when I . . . you know what . . . that ought to be interesting.

Chapter 1

Even before Claire Weiss died, Halloween was one of her favorite holidays, a close second only to Christmas. The draw: you got to dress up and pretend you were someone you weren't, someone famous or beautiful or exciting. Who wouldn't love that?

Except maybe someone who was already famous or beautiful or exciting.

Plus you got to eat all the candy you wanted. What a heavenly thing!

After Claire died, Halloween took on a whole new significance, this year even more so. After all, it wasn't every day that this Spirit American was allowed to come back to life.

Since this was her first attempt at reanimation, Claire figured there'd be a few hurdles to overcome, a bump or two in the road. Rumor had it reanimation was a rather complicated procedure. While in life she'd been considered intelligent by most standards, she had to admit she'd never been good at accomplishing complicated procedures of any sort. Even programming the universal remote control she'd purchased for her television two days before she'd passed away had been an extreme challenge—and a total waste of twelve bucks.

The process started out rather boring, like your typical day at the Secretary of State's office. Her arms loaded with a stack of pages, all blank except the bottom one, she stood in an endless line that seemed like it hadn't moved in eons. It stretched farther than the spirit eye could see, down past Cloud Nine, which was on the outer limits of purgatory.

She'd never complain about the line at a fast-food drive-through again! Speaking of which, one of her first stops would have to be Wendy's for one of those yummy shakes. And then a grocery store for some Ben & Jerry's . . . and a box of cordial cherries. Oh yeah . . .

She looked up in the general direction of the front then back toward the end. This was going to take forever. And nothing to read. No red scrolling signs like they had at her former credit union or TV playing Disney films like in her former hometown's post office. Not even some lame advertising posted on the walls.

When her catechism teacher had described purgatory as a nothing place, she hadn't been kidding. It was like a big fog cloud, not light, not dark. Just gray and plain and empty.

She glanced around again. Sheesh! The-Power-That-Be could've at least given a spirit something to stare at besides the back of the guy's head in front of her.

Bored to tears and figuring she would do her part to keep everyone around her from dying a horrific second death from boredom, she sang, "Devil with a blue dress, blue dress, blue dress. Devil with a blue dress on . . ."

Now there was a down-home kind of band. Put her in the going-home mood. The Detroit Wheels. Who couldn't love a band with a name like that?

The guy directly in front of her with the green-tinged toupee grunted. Grunted! The indignity.

Not sure if it was her voice that offended or the lyrics, she tried humming instead. The scowls continued. And

Mr. Green Toupee turned around and practically growled at her like a rabid dog.

Hey, she had no idea why that song, of all things, had stuck in her head. But she sure wouldn't judge someone based on what song was stuck in their head. To each his own, as she liked to say.

She didn't even comment on green toupees, at least not aloud. She sighed.

The line moved one step. Argh!

Would she get to the front of the line before *next* Halloween and miss out on reanimation completely? Maybe she should've gotten in line last year, or the year before that. The memo hadn't suggested she'd have any problems.

She tapped Mr. Green Toupee's shoulder. "Excuse me? Do you speak English? Am I in the right line? Is this one for those who passed in 1995?"

He mumbled an unfriendly "Yes."

"Do you know how long this'll take? I have some important business to take care of, some very pressing questions I'd like answered by a certain individual back on earth—"

"I wouldn't know."

The line moved one step forward. At this rate, she'd be waiting an eternity for her answers, never mind her chocolate fix!

Not the kind of person who'd handled waiting well, especially if it involved the delay of solving a mystery that had plagued her for nine long years, she looked to her right, at the line next to hers, for a distraction. She had to think about something else, pronto, or she'd go batty. To amuse herself, she checked out the clothes and hairstyles of those in the next line, trying to guess what year those souls had passed. Lots of leggings and big hair. Poor things! Had to be 1985. She wondered if they'd appreciate a little Madonna. "Like a virgin, hey!"

A young woman looked at Claire and rolled her eyes.

Time to check out the line on her left.

No doubt about it, those folks had passed away in the 1970s. They were even worse off style-wise than the 1980s group. Everyone sported polyester, bell bottoms, and platform shoes.

She felt fortunate. At least she'd passed away during a relatively normal fashion era, wouldn't be stuck reanimating in god-awful clothes she wouldn't be caught dead in . . .

I know. Bad joke.

"Attention, citizens," a deep voice boomed from some unseen source. "There is no waiting in the Express Line for those who know where they would like to reanimate and have all of their paperwork completed and signed by the appropriate parties."

She looked down at the stack of papers. It was signed. She bolted for the front, figuring she would find the Express Line once she got there.

As she ran, she felt like she was in a cartoon where the characters kept running and the scenery changed but they actually went nowhere. She ran past millions of patiently waiting souls. She ran for miles and miles—it was a good thing her spirit body was in better shape than her physical one had been or she'd have dropped dead of a heart attack.

Another bad joke.

Finally, she reached a long counter. Signs hung at regular intervals—1995, 1985, 1975, and so on. At the very end, way, way down, was a large sign that said, "Express." And there was no one waiting.

She dashed up, dropped her armload of paper on the counter and waited impatiently for a clerk, or angel, or whatever title they preferred to be called by, to come up and do what they had to do before sending her on her way.

A sweet little girl with big round eyes the color of Claire's favorite faded blue jeans and blond corkscrew curls that brushed her collarbones skipped up from some unseen place, tossed a rag doll onto the counter, and climbed up onto a tall bench. She wore the cutest little yellow dress with duckies on a wide bib collar. "Hi," she said in a sweet voice.

"Is . . . er, your mommy home?" Claire asked as she searched the gray nothingness behind the little girl for a door or escalator. Surely there was someone else on the way.

"My mother's still down below." She indicated a door to her left. "How can I help you?"

"I never imagined a little child would be working . . ." There had to be child-labor laws in purgatory, hadn't there? Could a child be trusted not to make a mistake? Claire couldn't afford to wake up in Outer Mongolia or . . . egad, the East Side of Detroit! "Sorry . . ."

"I'm used to it. Don't feel bad. Just put your worries at ease. I've been doing this job for seventy years now and I've been Employee of the Month for six months straight. I haven't made a mistake in decades."

"Impressive." Claire nodded. "I apologize again. I'm a nitwit." Ashamed for making such a big deal out of nothing, she pushed the stack of paper toward the little girl. "I'm here to apply for reanimation."

The child scrutinized every single page—how much could there be to read on a blank page? And speaking of reading, did she even know how to read?—before reaching the last one. "Everything looks in order. I'll need you to sign a few forms. Releases. Legal stuff, you know. Can't risk a lawsuit," she said gaily. Humming a song Claire didn't recognize, she produced an even higher stack out of the blue—literally—and dropped it on the counter and shoved it in Claire's direction. "Please read and initial every clause, then sign and date on the bottom line."

More blank papers? Was the copy machine broken?

"Um . . . I can't read this. There's nothing on the page. And I learned a long time ago not to sign any contract I haven't read thoroughly."

The little girl scooped up the papers, looked over Claire's shoulder and said, "I can help the next—"

"Hold up!" Claire interrupted. "You mean to tell me I lose my chance at reanimation if I merely question the terms of that contract?"

"Yes," the little girl said flatly. "The Almighty doesn't write an unjust contract. If you can't trust Him who can you trust?"

"You have a point. Give me that stack." She lifted the pen chained to the counter—there were pen-lifters in purgatory?—and started initialing each blank page, willy nilly, wherever she felt like it, then signed the bottom one and dated it October 31, 2004. "There you are. Let me guess, I just signed my life away."

"Something like that." The little girl scooped up the papers and shoved them on an unseen shelf below the counter, then handed Claire a small business card. "If you get yourself into trouble, call me."

"Are you my guardian angel?"

She giggled sweetly and hugged her doll. "Not hardly. Just your caseworker."

"Cool. My very own caseworker." Claire read the card. At least it had print she could read! *Bonnie Smith, Caseworker number 99956.*

This place had a real fixation with the number nine.

"Any phone'll work," Bonnie said as she stroked the yarn hair on her doll's head. "Just dial my worker number and you'll get through."

"Fair enough. Now what?" Claire asked, searching her clothes for a pocket. Finding none, she removed her feathered pink shoe and stowed the card in there. It might stink but it wouldn't get lost.

Bonnie set a small plastic cup, like the ones used to dispense medicine in the hospital, on the counter. "Swallow this."

Claire looked inside and swallowed out of reflex . . . and anxiety. "It's a horse pill. Surely I don't need such a large dose. Alive, I didn't weigh more than one-twenty—"

Bonnie grimaced and cleared her throat.

"Okay. Maybe one-thirty—"

Bonnie cleared her throat again.

"Okay, okay! You got me. Sheesh! A girl can't keep any secrets around here. One fifty-five."

"Believe me, you'll need every bit of this medicine. You wouldn't want to take too little. Take my word for it."

"Really? What happens?"

"You don't want to know. I'll put it this way: the results aren't pleasant." She poked an index finger at the cup. "Down you go."

"Don't I even get some water with it? I mean, it's bigger than a superduper multivitamin, for heaven's sake."

"Just take it." Bonnie pointed over Claire's shoulder. "The people behind you are waiting."

"Fine." Claire lifted the cup to her lips, opened her mouth, dumped the mammoth pill in, and tried to swallow.

Wham! A fiery blaze hit the back of her throat and she gasped. She felt like her entire neck was melting. Was that pill acid?

Wham! A second wave of pain hit her between the eyes and she clamped her eyelids closed. It felt like a red-hot poker had just drilled through her skull and was beating her brain into a puree.

Wham! A third blaze hit her in the belly and she dragged in a deep breath and yelled.

She heard her screams echo in nothingness. The beat of her heart thumped in her head, lub-dub . . . lub-dub . . . lub-dub . . .

She swallowed again, forcing the pill lower. The sound of her screams faded. Her heartbeat quickened. Lub-dub . . . lub-dub . . . lub-dub.

Then, bam! All kinds of sounds pummeled her eardrums. Fierce rumbling, screeching tires, dogs barking, wailing sirens. The sounds were so intense she feared her poor eardrums might burst. She covered the aching organs with her hands and blinked open her eyes.

Zap! The light was so bright she was sure it had burned her retinas. Her eyes teary, she immediately shut them again.

"Miss?" a loud voice boomed, even through her cupped hands. "Are you all right?"

Eyes closed, she nodded, hoping whoever was asking would just let her be, wherever she was, in peace. Or at least not talk again. His voice felt like the roar of a jet engine as it pummeled her poor system.

Her throat still burning, she swallowed again.

Evidently not about to let her wallow in agony in peace, he belted her in the shoulder—or rather, that's how his touch felt. "Miss? Should I call an ambulance?"

"Oh, God no," her voice resonated in her head so loudly she cringed. "The sirens would kill me. I'll . . . be fine. In a minute," she lied, sure she would be curled up on the cold ground, hands clapped over her ears for a long, long time.

Where had she landed? Hell? Every sensation was excruciatingly intense. Sounds drilled through her body like a jackhammer. Touches blasted her nerves like powerful blows. Light scorched her eyes, giving her an instant migraine.

Her throat still burned. It felt like the pill was lodged midway between her mouth and her stomach. She concentrated on swallowing, over and over again. Slowly, the pain in her throat descended lower . . . lower . . . As it moved, the intensity of the sensations faded. Encouraged, she swallowed quickly again and again. Finally, when the sounds around her didn't make her teeth ache, she tried opening her eyes again.

She recognized where she was. That was a good sign. At least she wasn't in hell, as she'd feared, or the East Side.

A cold gust blasted her as she stood, making her shiver. She blinked as she looked up and down the street. The hazy, amber light of a streetlamp illuminated a small area of road and sidewalk. A line of dumpy little shops, crammed tightly next to each other and crowding the street, were dark and lifeless, with one exception: the brick-faced building a half-block down. In its window a tired neon sign flickered, advertising the establishment's name, Devil's Night.

She'd made it!

"Well, that wasn't so bad. Although I have a new respect for my mother. After that agony, I can just imagine what childbirth was like. No wonder she had only me."

She stood, stretched, and tested her legs with a few wobbly steps.

Yeppers. No doubt about it. She was alive, in the flesh . . . and . . . uh-oh! . . . needing a wardrobe change. For a moment, she'd forgotten what she had on.

Thankful for the unseasonably warm weather, which wasn't even close to warm enough, considering she was wearing a cute matching babydoll nightie and robe made out of the lightest material known to mankind, she dashed down the sidewalk—or rather half staggered, half stumbled. Evidently it took a few minutes to get the hang of walking again.

Chilled, she ducked through the first unlocked door she found. Devil's Night had been her favorite weekend hangout, a dingy nightclub that hosted live bands on Friday and Saturday nights.

Time to put step one of her plan into action.

Chapter 2

Claire staggered into the building and struggled to catch her breath—not a good move in a smoky nightclub. The irritating toxins burned her delicate lungs, causing her to break into a spastic coughing fit. She sounded like her aunt Jeanne after she took a drag from her first Camel cigarette every morning.

Once the violent choking and gasping settled and the subsequent tears cleared from her eyes, she took a look around.

Dark, loud, smelly, and crowded. Those were the words that would best describe Devil's Night. It definitely wasn't the nicest place on earth, but part of its charm was in the people who frequented the dump. Bikers with long scraggly hair and clothing bearing skulls and crossbones, desperate forty-something women who knew the statistics regarding their chances of finding a man and were willing to do anything to be an exception to the rule, an assortment of two-timing low-life middle-class bastards who weren't satisfied by their beautiful trophy wives at home. . . .

Okay, it was one person in particular that gave this dump its charm.

Claire had a lot of regrets in life. Since she'd died young, as her parents and grandparents before her, she'd left behind a lengthy to-do list, including finishing the bachelor's degree she'd never completed, having a child, traveling to Europe, and sleeping with Jake Faron.

With only nine days available to her, most of the unfinished business on that list would remain unchecked. But that final one, well, that was one she could do something about, assuming she could find him. At least she was starting in the right place and on the right night.

In the five years she'd been going to this bar, she had noticed one thing: Jake never missed a Thursday night.

And here it was Thursday night. How convenient.

Just inside the door, Claire pressed her back against the rough paneled wall and continued to scope out the scene. After all this time she would've expected some changes, some new faces at least, maybe a different band. But things looked very much like they had the last time she'd been there.

You people are stuck in a rut.

Yes, she was there too, in that dump, on maybe the only night she'd be alive for the next decade, and it was pathetic, but she had taken nine years off—never mind the fact that she hadn't had a choice. It didn't look like these folks had missed a Ladies Night since the last time she'd been there.

Besides, she was there tonight for one very important reason.

She wanted to get laid.

Okay, that didn't sound so original. Huh. Oh well.

As she'd hoped—and planned for—the bar was hosting their usual Devil's Night bash. Everyone, including Bob the bartender and Melissa and Janet, the waitresses, was dressed in costumes. Almost all the women wore sexy, skimpy numbers. The place was stuffed to the gills with genies, mermaids, sexy nurses, French maids, and the like. It was hard to imagine, but Claire's skimpy nightgown looked a little tame compared to the outfits on most of the ladies.

So much for being embarrassed.

A little relieved—there were still a lot of reasons to be nervous—she ventured farther into the bar, scanning the crowd for Jake. He had to be there. Somewhere. At his favorite table in the back, by the dartboards, she hoped.

Please, let tonight not be the first Thursday night he's missed in who knows how long. Wouldn't that be my luck?

While she had been able to control where she reanimated, she hadn't been able to influence several other factors, like what she was wearing—she appeared in the same clothes she'd worn when she passed. She also had no control over the weather or where other people would be.

As a result, she'd done her best to plan for the worst while hoping for the best. So far, so good. But if she didn't find Jake, all of her more pleasant plans would go down the drain.

No matter how creative you got, some things just weren't possible without a partner.

Her heart hopping around like a jackrabbit in her chest—she'd forgotten how funny that felt—she pushed her way through the crowd of nearly naked women and drooling men, toward his table.

It was empty. Darn! Now what? Nine long, boring, sexless years of planning wasted!

Maybe Jake had gotten a life, moved on, maybe even married and fathered a flock of kids. There was no way for her to know for sure. She knew only one thing: his table was empty. It showed no signs whatsoever of him. No clear plastic boxes for his darts or empty Labatt Blue bottles. No black leather jacket or mangled paper napkins. Not even a cigar butt in the ashtray.

It was empty, clean, unused.

Now, that was strange. Considering the place resembled a fully packed sardine can, and every other table was stacked with pizza dishes, beer bottles, and cocktail glasses, this one empty, sparkling-clean table seemed out of place.

"Excuse me," a familiar deep, husky voice said behind her, giving birth to happy little goosebumps all over her arms and shoulders. She'd forgotten how funny those felt too.

It had to be him!

This was it, her one chance. Her only chance. A once-in-an-eternity chance. It had to work.

Sweet Jesus, she was nervous! Hot and cold at the same time, she felt a sheen of sweat coat her skin instantly. And thanks to her racing heart, she wondered if she might jump right out of her newly acquired body.

She took a split second to compose herself. A couple of deep breaths did absolutely no good.

"Excuse me," he repeated a little more loudly.

That was her cue. Time to turn around.

He tapped her shoulder yet she couldn't budge. "Miss?"

Turn around, dummy. She couldn't move a muscle. Frozen stiff as frogs caught in a late spring ice storm—those things happened in Michigan—out of plain fear. What if he didn't recognize her? Or what if he did know who she was but didn't care?

So what! I didn't go through the agony of reanimation to wimp out. Turn around now! Turn around, turn around, turn around.

His frustrated sigh, combined with the obnoxious chant that kept reverberating through her head, was enough to force her to twist her body ever so slightly to the right. She slowly turned her head. . . .

Wow. He didn't look a day older than the last time she'd seen him, except for maybe a few more gray hairs in the dark sideburns, which made him even sexier than she remembered. Same square jaw with a couple days' stubble.

Same eyes that were too blue to be real, same dark curly hair, same muscle-mag body.

She sighed.

"Claire?" His eyebrows rose to comical heights.

So, she'd managed to surprise him. But would he be pleased?

"Yep, it's me. In the flesh." She completed her turn, then threw in a three-sixty for good measure, just in case he'd forgotten what he was missing. A girl had to take every advantage available in the quest for no-strings sex.

His gaze dropped for a split second to approximately chest level, then zipped right back up to her face. His lop-sided smile was an encouraging sign. "I'd say so. How've you been? It's been a long, long time. What? At least six years?"

"Nine, actually. I've been good. Thanks. And you?" She tried to check his ring finger but as usual his hand was stuffed into his jacket pocket.

"Good, thanks." His gaze wandered up and down her body again and the smile that hadn't faded grew broader, even gained a naughty little glint.

Her face burned with a blush. Other parts burned too.

"You look fantastic," he said, his voice like a low, rumbly purr. For the first time since she'd turned around, his gaze left her, but only for a split second. "Don't tell me you're here alone."

"Yes, I am."

He looked pleased with her response. "Then I insist you join me. I'm anxious to hear what you've been up to for the past nine years. Looks like my table's empty." His hand dropped to her waist as he gently steered her toward the cozy booth in the corner.

Almost too thrilled to speak, she walked to the table. It was no easy task her scooting sweaty legs across the red vinyl-covered bench, at least not without sounding like she'd had too much Taco Bell for dinner, but she did the best she could. Since he was wearing a pair of jeans that hugged his butt tighter than any inanimate object had the right to, a white t-shirt, and his signature black leather, he didn't suffer the same difficulties she did.

Once they were comfy and cozy—Claire had never been any cozier—he removed his jacket and tossed it into the corner, then flagged down Janet, the waitress. "What'll you have?" he asked Claire.

The last thing she wanted was to waste her one night on earth getting drunk, barfing for hours, and passing out. Dead or not, she'd kick her own butt if she goofed and ended up missing this opportunity. For one thing, she couldn't get any answers about her death until midnight tomorrow. If she didn't get the chance to talk to her ex-fiancé she'd suffer another ten long years of wondering why she'd been shot.

Besides, she felt like she needed to clear the air with him since she'd died in his bed, yet she wasn't interested in pursuing anything with him during her short visit to earth. She kind of hoped he'd found someone new and settled down.

"It's been a while since I've had anything stronger than water," she said. "I'd better stick with a diet cola."

Janet, dressed in a very short, extremely tight nurse's uniform that didn't exactly cover her butt or boobs, smiled at Claire as she wrote down her order.

"Are you sure?" Jake asked. After waiting for Claire's decisive nod, he said, "I'll have a Labatt Blue."

"Sure thing, Jake. It's good seeing both of you again. It's been a long time," Janet said. "Your table's been empty since the last time you were here, Jake. It's like no one wants to sit in it."

"You haven't been here in a while either?" Claire asked, surprised.

"No. Neither have you?" he asked.

"Nope. I guess I got lucky tonight," she thought aloud.

He gave her the kind of straight-in-the-eye stare you see only in the movies, which made breathing regularly a bit of a challenge. "I was about to say the same thing," he whispered.

"Uh . . . I . . . oh . . ." Where was her drink? Her tongue had glued itself to the roof of her mouth! In all the years she'd known Jake Faron—if you could call an occasional friendly smile in passing or brief exchange of pleasantries *knowing* someone—he'd never once looked at her like that. Like she was the triple-fudge-cake-with-ice-cream-and-hot-chocolate-sauce piece of sin on the dessert cart that a person might secretly yearn for but would never have the guts to order.

She had the sneaking suspicion she wouldn't be waiting another nine years to get what she was hoping for, at least in one respect.

But first things first. She needed to make sure she'd be around for the next several days to take care of some other things. How did one touch someone's heart when they were practically a stranger? Touching other parts was no problem, especially considering how close he was sitting. With just the slightest reach, she could easily touch his . . . oh . . . that was one promising bulge.

Sheesh! She needed to get her mind out of the man's pants and concentrate on her current challenge. In life, she'd touched many a person's heart with even a small show of kindness. A bouquet of flowers to a sick relative. A few hours babysitting for a single mom so she could go to the grocery store or just enjoy some private time in peace. A trip to the veterinarian with a sick pet.

She needed some information: background stuff, family, work, anything. Did he have any pets? She was especially good at being nice to animals. "What's new?"

"Nothing much. How about you?"

"How's your job?" she asked, purposefully avoiding

answering his question. She felt like a journalist digging for the big story, or a detective.

"Um . . . Work's work. Yours?"

Give me something to work with here. I promise you won't be sorry. "Good. Your mother? Father? Grandparents? Great aunts? Distant cousins by marriage?"

"I don't . . . they all passed away when I was young."

"Oh." Well, this line of questioning was getting her nowhere. She needed either another strategy or another victim. "I'm so sorry."

"It's just as well. . . ." he said, not finishing his sentence when Janet brought their drinks. He gave the waitress a stunner of a smile and asked, "Can you put that on my tab?"

"Sure." Janet shook her finger at him. "Just promise me you won't stiff me like you did last time." She winked and bounced away, saying over her shoulder, "Just kidding. I trust you."

"Now," he said, returning his attention to Claire, "what about you?" He twisted the top off his beer and took several long swallows. His tongue darted out and licked a droplet of glistening wetness from his lower lip.

"Hmm?" Not listening as closely as she knew she should, she stared at those lips, wondering if they'd taste as wonderful as they looked. They were so cute, the way the upper one curved. . . .

"Your family?" He took another swallow, then set the beer on the table.

"Oh." She shook her head to clear it and took a few much-needed gulps of her cola. As usual it was lukewarm. She felt herself scowling.

"Warm?" he asked, nodding. "I should've warned you."

She chuckled and forced herself to take another drink. Warm or not, she needed the liquids to keep her mouth from drying out—darned, wonderful, troublesome nerves. "I should've remembered. I've never once had a cold glass of cola in this joint. My family, you ask? They're gone too. My family has this curse. We all die young."

"I'm sorry too." He looked as regretful as a guy could look when he was talking to a girl in a nightie.

"Pets? Do you have any animals? I love animals. Haven't met a dog or cat that didn't like me—except my own," she added, chuckling as she recalled Gulliver's reaction when she'd first passed. It had been classic and if she hadn't been so freaked out about seeing her poor body lying in a puddle of blood on the bed she'd shared with then-fiancé, Matt Gerald, she might have found it amusing.

That night, she learned a lot of things—too bad it ended in her demise. Then again, that shouldn't have surprised her. She'd always been the kind of person who had to learn things the hard way.

"I did, once. I had a dog named Rambo," he said after polishing off his beer.

"Let me guess. It was a German shepherd. Or a Rottweiler? Something big and tough."

"No, actually Rambo was a poodle," he admitted with a guilty smile.

She laughed. Couldn't help herself. The picture of this black-leather-clad, tight-jeaned man walking a fluffy little poodle was too funny not to laugh at. "Was it a black poodle? For some reason, I'm imagining him black. Maybe wearing one of those little leather dog coats."

He didn't seem to mind her reaction. In fact, he joined in her laughter. "No, he was white. But believe me, Rambo was the baddest miniature poodle, with a light blue bow on his little ball-topped head, that ever walked the earth."

"I'm sure he was," she said, trying like heck to sober herself. It took several gulps of warm diet cola to do the trick. "I couldn't help noticing, you said 'had' not 'have'."

"Yeah. He's gone too. I really miss him. Got him from the Humane Society."

"Well, aren't we a pitiful pair, then? No friends, family, or even pets to speak of."

"Your cat gone too?"

"He ran away when I . . . um, never mind. Let's put it this way, he didn't handle change very well."

"I'm sorry. I've heard that about cats."

"Yeah."

Silence. Time to shift gears, lighten the mood. She polished off her warm diet cola, then gave him one of her most seductive smiles. Forget about the touching-the-heart thing. She was trying too hard. It would happen when it happened and with whomever. If not Jake, then with someone else. She just needed to go with the flow. "I don't know why we never sat down and talked like this before."

"The word on the street was you were engaged," he said.

Oh yeah. How could I forget? "Yes, I was. But I'm not engaged anymore. We . . . er . . . parted ways a long time ago. I guess you could say our lives took us in different directions, not that there are any bad feelings between us or anything. Honestly, I haven't spoken to him in a long time." Sensing he was getting uncomfortable, she steered the topic away from her past lovers by adding, "I'm not married either, in case that was your next question."

A brief smile flashed across his face, quickly replaced by a more sober expression. He scooted closer, draped an arm over her shoulder, and with his other hand patted her thigh in a show of consolation. "That's gr . . . I'm sorry to hear it didn't work out."

She gazed into his eyes.

Just tell him the truth and quit with the small talk. Tell him how you feel.

Her palms slicker than a slug, her heart galloping faster than the horses in the Kentucky Derby, she dragged in a deep breath and said, "I've been very lonely. I've been thinking about you—"

The band chose that moment to start their first set. A very bad rendition of "Tainted Love" blared from the enormous speakers sitting on either side of the stage, making every particle of air in the place vibrate.

So much for her big confession. And she'd been doing so well, and was just about to seal the deal!

That was okay. She didn't need to speak to get her point across. Thanks to her theatrical experience—so it was in high school; you never forgot those things—nonverbal communication was one of her most practiced skills. She dried her palms on the bottom of her nightgown, adjusted the neckline to emphasize two of her best features—the right one and the left one—then reached for his hand and twined her fingers in his and lifted her hand to her chest.

His expression a mixture of indecision and out-and-out lust, he studied her for a brief moment, then shouted, "You want to go somewhere quiet?"

"Absolutely."

He leaned over her as he reached for his jacket. The proximity to such delicious hunkiness made her every sense come alive. He smelled of aftershave and man and fresh October air. The dark stubble on his jaw scratched across her shoulder as he caught his jacket in his fist and dragged it closer. Despite the eardrum-shattering music, she heard the sound of her own gasp when his lips brushed across the back of her neck.

"How about your place?" His jacket wadded in a ball, he scooted out from behind the table and stood. "Mine's . . . a . . . a mess." He offered her a hand as she struggled to scoot across the bench. At least with the music, she didn't have to worry about making obscene noises.

"Shucks. I'd like to invite you to my apartment but that's kind of a problem." She stood in front of him on shaky legs that had no reason to be so unsteady, outside of the obvious. "I'm open for suggestions."

Shit! She sounded so lame she was tempted to club herself in the head. He probably thought she was lying, or married, despite having said otherwise. Why hadn't she planned for the *where* when she'd planned the *who*, *what*, and *when*? All this time she'd assumed he would be more than willing to take her back to his place.

Stupid, stupid, stupid!

She checked her clothes for a stash of money. Surely He—meaning the All-Knowing Creator of the Universe—wouldn't send her down to earth penniless!

Okay, He did.

Would it be tacky to suggest Jake pay for a hotel? For nine days? No good. She'd need to find another alternative. Fast!

Think, think, think! Before he gets suspicious and bolts.

Chapter 3

If he hadn't passed away once already, Jake Faron would have sworn he'd just died and gone to heaven. Things couldn't have gone any more smoothly if he'd planned it. There she was, the woman he'd waited way too many years to speak with. The woman he had wasted more than five years watching from afar, waiting, wondering.

He'd been a damn fool!

If only he'd known he would bite the big one only a handful of nights after the last time he'd seen her—nine stinking long years ago—he would've been more courageous. Actually, he'd almost said something. He'd planned it out, rehearsed what he wanted to say. But that Wednesday morning, the day before he was going to approach her with his confession, he'd woken up, showered, and swallowed his protein bar, never thinking he would die before he arrived at the office.

A train derailed as he sat at a railroad crossing less than a half-mile from his home. One of the cars fell over, landing on top of his SUV and killing him instantly. There were some things even a Hummer couldn't protect a guy from.

Physically, dying didn't hurt a bit. Too many endorphins in the system to shut down the nerve endings. But emotionally, it was excruciating—more painful than reanimation.

He had too many regrets to pass peacefully from the world of the physical to the world of the spirit. The biggest: being a damned chicken shit. He shouldn't have let that fruitcake Claire had been engaged to stop him from going to her. He should've had some balls. He should've gone up to her long ago, told her how he felt, and taken her to his bed . . . where he could show her.

Should've, should've, should've.

Instead, he'd been the guy his mother had raised him to be: honorable to a fault. He'd silently watched her fall in love with a man who didn't deserve to clean the mud from her tires. He died before he found out if she'd actually gone through with the wedding.

A quick check of her left hand tonight had confirmed what she'd told him. If she did, in fact, marry that schmuck, she'd done the intelligent thing and divorced him. And lucky for her, although he assumed if they'd been married she'd given that bastard as many as nine years of her life, she looked like she hadn't aged a day.

When he'd reanimated tonight, he'd come to this dump hoping beyond hope she might by some miracle show up. It had been a long shot. Lady Luck was smiling on him! He should pay a visit to the horse tracks tonight too.

Either that or Someone was intervening on his behalf. He glanced up at the smoke-clogged ceiling and mouthed a silent thank you, then looked down at the woman he cherished, the woman he would wait an eternity to make love to, if necessary.

She shifted uncomfortably from one foot to the other and he ached with the need to wipe away every ounce of tension he saw on her face. Yet, at the moment, he lacked the means to do anything to ease her worries, whatever they might be. No money. No credit cards. No access to a car. How could he help her with anything? Hell, he couldn't think of a place to take her so they could enjoy some quiet time together.

Memories of his high school days, when he was trying to come up with a plan to bone his girlfriend, Missy, came to mind. He'd been desperate and horny. A buggy, itchy haystack in an old dilapidated barn behind the school's football field had been good enough then. He didn't expect Claire to accept those kinds of conditions now.

Damn it! He'd wanted tonight to be so special, for her sake. Busted, with no wheels and no place to go, that wasn't looking likely.

Shit! Maybe this had been a bad idea. So what if he told her how he felt? There wasn't anything either one of them could do about it now. At best, he'd be around for nine days, at worst one. In the end, he'd only hurt her.

"I'd better get going," he said. "Maybe another time."

"Hold up!" For a little thing, she had a strong grip. Her fingers wrapped around his wrist and squeezed more tightly than an overly friendly anaconda. "I've waited a long time to come here and talk to you—"

Did he hear her right or had the obnoxious 80s cover tunes the band was playing distorted her words? "You've been waiting to talk to me?"

"Yes, and I'm not going to let you skate outta here so easy. I may not've planned this well—"

"Planned what?"

"Let's go outside where we don't have to shout." She tugged on his arm as she pushed her way through the crowd. Despite her best efforts, they didn't get far very fast. After they'd traveled no more than two steps, his sense of pride and pity for the wiry little woman who was trying mightily to shove aside a guy at least three times her size took over and he swapped places with her, leading the way outside.

She was a little disheveled by the time they got outside but her mussed hair and off-kilter nightgown only added to her charm.

Damn, she was sexy. He stared at a bare shoulder and imagined himself snuggling up next to her in bed every night. Too bad the best he could hope for was nine nights every ten years.

Death just wasn't fair.

"So, what is this about planning?" he asked when he found his tongue. He could've sworn it wasn't in his mouth a minute ago. The damn thing had probably been dragging on the ground.

She followed the line of his gaze and self-consciously pulled the flimsy, translucent robe back in place. "I . . . came here tonight hoping to see you." Her face changed in color from soft pink to a darker rose. It was a nice contrast to her soft blond hair, cool gray eyes, and barely pink, almost flesh-toned negligee. "I know it's been a long time and we haven't really sat down and talked much before tonight, but I was hoping . . . I mean I was wondering if you might . . . Shit."

"Huh? You want me to shit? Here?" he teased.

She shook her head, crossed her arms over her chest, and lowered her chin, grumbling, "Pathetic. I must be the world's worst seductress."

Seductress? Out here it couldn't be the loud music distorting her words. He had to have heard her correctly. Just in case, he figured he'd better double-check. "Is that what you're trying to do? Seduce me?"

"See?" She threw her hands in the air in the universal sign of frustration. Then she sighed and wrapped her arms back around her body. "You don't even know I was trying to seduce you. How sad is that?"

"Are you cold?" he asked, noting her stiff posture.

"A little."

He wrapped his coat around her shoulders. "Better?"

She nodded, then poked her arms through the sleeves. "Thanks." She looked comical. The sleeves hung past her fingertips. The shoulders slouched half-way down her arms. The waist skimmed the tops of her thighs, making her look like she had no clothes on underneath. Just the jacket and pink feathered, high heeled mules. "I feel so stupid."

He followed her long, slender legs to her feather covered toes, then let his gaze slowly climb back up again. "Stupid? Why? Maybe I didn't see what you were trying to do. But it doesn't mean I wouldn't appreciate it if you were."

"Stop. I don't like being patronized." Her sharp gaze challenged him to come clean. Problem was, he was telling the truth.

"I'm not patronizing you. I'm serious," he said.

"You're a bad liar."

"You wound me! Shoot, I would never lie to a woman about something so sensitive." He threw his hands up in the air. "Go ahead, seduce me. Please. Take my word for it, I won't stop you."

She made no move toward him.

Guess she doesn't believe me.

"Oh puh-leez. You look about as thrilled as the last guy I dragged to the opera . . . on Super Bowl Sunday."

He laughed. Funny, sexy, smart, with a sharp wit. Claire was delightful, not that he was surprised. "Is this better?" He concentrated on giving her the most aroused, hot gaze he could muster. Even though he was turned on by both her lovely body and her charm, he was having a hard time making it apparent on his face. It wasn't something a guy did consciously. When he thought he had it nailed, he murmured, "Come on, baby. Give me your best shot."

She laughed, not the reaction he was hoping for. "That's even worse. Now you look like you're straining on the toilet."

Despite a twinge of embarrassment, he joined in her

laughter. It felt wonderful to laugh. Energy charged through his system, making him feel even more alive. "I don't do well with an audience. Guess I'd make a cruddy porn star. But believe me, I'm hot . . . for you," he added, in case there might be any doubt what or who was making him hot.

"Right. You don't exactly look like you're about to lose control and take me right here on the street."

"I have a great poker face. Ask the boys. Honestly, I'm doing my best to contain myself but I can stop trying if you want me to."

"Shut up." She swung a sleeve at him but missed by a mile. "You're just saying that to be nice."

If only she knew. He'd forgotten how uncomfortable a hard-on could be. He needed to adjust his jockeys, or get rid of them altogether. "I can prove it if you like."

"How?" When he motioned to the lump at the front of his pants, her mouth formed a perfect oval. "Oh . . ."

"I figured I'd do my part to keep us from going to jail for indecent exposure or whatever bonking in the streets is called."

Her cheeks took on a very sexy pink hue, again. "Good thinking. That's the last thing I need tonight."

"So, what's the occasion?" He grabbed her upper arms and pulled her toward him. He'd had enough of the joking around. It was time to get down to business, even if they were standing outside. His balls weren't going to let this go on much longer. A kiss wouldn't get them hauled off to jail.

"Occasion?" she croaked, visibly swallowing.

"What occasion are we celebrating?" Not waiting for her to answer, he lowered his head until his mouth pressed against hers.

Sweet Loving Jesus! Was he dying again? There were too many sensations. It was too intense.

As his tongue explored the sweet depth of her mouth,

he felt her body sagging against his, her arms reaching up and looping around his neck, the quick, uneven thump of his heart. The softness of her belly pressed against his rigid rod.

He heard her sigh and his groan, smelled the fruity scent of her shampoo. Even better, he tasted her, drank from her with a thirst he was sure would never be sated.

What a way to go! As his tongue slid along hers, caressing, tasting, he let his hands slide downward, following her torso to the bottom of his jacket. There, they crept around her back until his fingers touched the skin of her thighs. A little shift upward and he found pay dirt in the form of a soft, round rear end covered in flimsy material.

If he were in any other place besides a busy street, he would've torn away those panties and explored what lay beneath. His balls tightened more. Oh, the agony!

Dizzy from forgetting to breathe, he broke the kiss and looked down into Claire's heavily lidded eyes. "We need to go."

"Where?" she whispered.

"Somewhere. Anywhere. I . . ." He tried to think, tried to come up with an idea, but thanks to that kiss, his synapses weren't exactly meeting. He looked up the street. No idea. He looked down the street. Still no idea.

He looked into her eyes . . . His hard-on grew more urgent. He gritted his teeth. Things were getting desperate.

If only he could give his buddy John a call. A freelance photographer who was out of town as much as he was in, he had a place a couple of blocks away, a studio apartment he used part-time to crash when he wasn't away on shoots. Jake couldn't count the number of times he'd staggered there to sleep off the effects of a few too many at Devil's Night.

"Wonder if John's on a job?" he thought aloud.

"John?"

"Where's your car?" he asked.

"I . . . uh . . . came with a friend. But she had to leave. Babysitter problems. Where's yours?"

"The shop. I . . . er . . . walked here. No matter. I think I know a place we can go. It's just a short walk." He wrapped his arm around her shoulder and led her down the street, hoping, praying, and wishing John's apartment was empty and his refrigerator was full. After loving Claire to the moon and back and doing his kind deed to insure he'd be around for the next eight nights to do it over and over and over again, he was going to need a nice big meal.

Chapter 4

"Hold up." Suddenly uncomfortable, Claire dug her heels into the sidewalk. Considering she was wearing high heels, the results were less than satisfactory.

"What's wrong?" Jake asked, looking guilty as hell.

"Call me crazy, but something's not right." She forced herself to look away from him because it was too hard to concentrate. He had the most amazing eyes she'd ever seen. Dark, almost black, with eyelashes not even Maybelline could give a girl. "First you tell me you don't have a car and you don't know where to take me. Then out of the blue you come up with an idea, just like that." She snapped her fingers to illustrate. "You want to take me to some guy John's house. And wouldn't you know it? He lives right around the block. How convenient."

"And that's suspicious?"

"Kind of. I don't know . . . something's not right. Why would you forget your friend lives right around the block?"

"Because I haven't seen him in a while?"

"I haven't seen my friends for nine years, but I still remember where they live. It must be something else. Let me guess . . . um . . . Oh, I got it. You're an undercover cop and I'm being busted for solicitation. Shoot, how can I be so stupid? It was the nightie, wasn't it?"

"I'm not an undercover cop. Whatever gave you that idea?"

"I should've seen it coming," Claire continued as she paced back and forth nervously. "We've been going to the same club for years. Yet you never once looked at me like that before. Nothing more than a friendly nod and a 'hey, how you doing?' and all of a sudden you can't keep your hands off me? Then you tell me you don't have a car. That it's in the shop. You drive a Hummer, for God's sake. Nothing breaks those, not even a tank."

"A train would."

"Well, obviously you haven't been run over by a train recently. Your hair looks too good . . . every part of you for that matter." She looked up and down the street, expecting to see a horde of men running toward her. But the street remained empty. "So, when's the team going to jump out of their hiding spots and ambush me?"

"What team?"

"You know, the SWAT team or whatever those guys are called. The ones that bust prostitutes. I've watched them on TV." She spied a large white van across the street and waved. The high-tech communication gear was always in a big white van. "Come on out, guys. I know what's coming, but you've got it all wrong. I'm innocent . . . well, not exactly. The only virgin in my house was in an olive oil bottle, but I'm far from a prostitute." She looked at Jake. "Why aren't they coming? And why haven't you slapped a set of cuffs on me and pinned me up against a car? Am I going to be on TV? One of those cool police shows? Make sure they don't blur out my face. I'll take my fifteen minutes of fame any way I can get it." She waved again and mouthed *Hi Mom*. "Where's the hidden camera? I want to make sure the cameraman gets my good side."

"There isn't a camera. There isn't a SWAT team. But I might be able to do something about the cuffs if you like.

And I have my own opinion about which side is your best one."

"Honest? There's no camera?"

"I swear on my mother's grave."

"No TV show?"

"Sorry to disappoint you."

Despite being bummed out because she wasn't going to be on TV—another one of those unfinished tasks she never thought she would accomplish—she shuddered at the thought of being handcuffed to Jake's bed. "Do I dare ask which side you think is best?"

He answered her with a swat on her rump that stung just enough to make her smile.

Who cared about TV! "Which way to John's house?" she asked, satisfied she wasn't going to be thrown in jail for solicitation.

"Just down a couple blocks." He took her hand in his hand and squeezed, cocking his head and giving her a wicked smile that made her toes curl. "This way."

As they walked, they released each other's hands and strolled with their bodies pressed side by side. It was dark. The streets were empty with the exception of a few stray cats digging through trash containers and yowling at the moon. The sky was clear of clouds, boasting millions of twinkling stars. It was the perfect atmosphere for—sigh—romance.

Walking silently, she let her hand roam down, over Jake's bottom, then up his back and around to what chest she could reach. His hands were far from stationary too. Thanks to tickles, touches, and little moans of pleasure, Claire felt like she was going to melt by the time they arrived at John's apartment, a little upper flat above an art gallery.

Nine years of waiting was coming to an end! She'd never anticipated sex with so much enthusiasm. Based on what she saw already, she knew she wouldn't be disappointed. Jake had some wicked, wicked hands and a deep voice that reverberated in her belly and released more endorphins than a bucket of chocolate.

Jake gave the wooden door a couple of sound knocks, loud enough to alert the apartment's sleeping inhabitant.

They shared a couple of naughty gropes and heated gazes as they waited for an answer.

There had better be no one home! Claire was sure she'd combust if she had to wait much longer. Her panties were wringing wet. The thin material cooled as the slightest breeze blew on it. The effect was dizzying. Cool wetness on hot flesh.

He gave the door a couple more knocks and then started walking down the sidewalk. He held out his hand and she put hers in it, letting him lead her down the street toward a narrow alley. "This way."

"Are you sure it's safe?" Horny as heck, but nervous at the same time, she glanced around the urban landscape, looking for potential assailants, muggers, etc. This wasn't the best part of town, even if it was a suburb of Detroit. It would suck to be murdered a second time on, potentially, her one night on Earth. What a bummer that would be!

"It's been a while since I've been down here, and no place is one-hundred-percent safe, but I'm keeping my eyes open. It's always been pretty quiet." He checked the dark alley, just narrow enough to squeeze a body between the two tall buildings. There was a black metal gate at the entry. He tried it. Locked.

"Shoot. I hope I still have the key. John never used to lock this gate." He rummaged through his jeans pocket and produced a key ring loaded with at least a dozen keys. He slid one into the lock and gave it a twist and the gate swung open with a gentle nudge. "I have a key to the back door," he explained as he motioned for her to pass through the gate first. He followed her, pushing it shut and securing the lock behind them.

Thankful for the security that the hulking man behind her, the light of a little bare bulb and the locked gate gave her, she walked with relatively little fear down the alley, humming "Let's Go All the Way" as she stared straight ahead. The alley led to a tiny, walled-in back garden that was much too pretty to be sitting in the middle of such an ugly urban setting.

"How cute."

"My buddy has the greenest thumb I've ever seen." Jake motioned toward an arbor. "This way." He motioned for her to precede him. "By the way, what song is that you're humming?"

"Oh, just some stupid eighties tune. I'm sure you've never heard it, since I'm guessing you were into heavy metal."

He grinned as he slid the key into the backdoor lock and gave the knob a twist. "You sure make a lot of assumptions." He pushed open the door and poked his head in. "Hey, John? You home?" he shouted. Then he motioned for her to enter.

She liked that grin of his, she realized as she brushed against him to step into the tiny cramped landing of a steep staircase. That wicked smile made the kind of promises she'd waited a long time for. "I have an active imagination," she murmured suggestively.

He pulled the door closed behind him and secured the lock. "So do I. Ladies first."

She was not disappointed when he took advantage of his position behind her to grope her bottom as she climbed the staircase. Her kitty purred as he cupped her butt cheeks and lifted slightly, a fingertip tracing the leg band of her panties.

"You smell amazing," he said in a low growl that made her shiver with delight.

Her legs the consistency of unbaked cookie dough, she stopped at the top of the stairs and waited for him to tell her what to do. Should she just try the door?

His full length pressed against her back, Jake reached around her to open it. "John, are you here?" There was no answer. "Looks like we're in luck." He pushed the door completely open and stepped inside. It was pitch black. "Wait right there. I'll switch on a light." Then she heard a crash and "Ouch! Shit!" A few more bumps and thuds. "Damn it. Owww!"

"It's okay. Maybe we should just forget about the light. Who needs it? Heck, you probably wouldn't want to see my fat—"

"John must've gotten all new furniture. I can't find a thing in the dark. Oh, wait. I think this might be a lamp."

A dim light pierced a small, golden hole in the inky black.

Claire blinked. Even though it wasn't exactly the brightest light she'd ever seen, it was a sharp contrast to the dark they'd been standing in for quite some time. Fortunately it took only a second or two for her eyes to adjust.

The first thing she did was a quick visual check of Jake for any signs of life-threatening injury. "Are you okay?" she asked as she stepped closer.

The pink stain on his cheeks and neck was simply too cute for words. "I'm fine. It's just a little scratch and maybe a minor concussion," he said, rubbing his left forearm and head at the same time, a comical sight. "Sorry. I shouldn't have cussed." Wincing, he stooped over and picked up a broken picture frame off the floor, then lifted a jagged piece of mirrored glass with the other hand. "Looks like we're in for seven years bad luck."

"Not a problem about the cussing," she said with a chuckle. "Believe me, I've said worse." She reached out and ran her hand down his chest, down over lumpy abs she couldn't wait to see, and stopped at his belt. "Don't you think you should put down that dangerous glass? You wouldn't want to cut yourself. And we can talk about our bad luck later. After we check and see if John bought himself some new *bedroom* furniture. . . ."

The pink deepened to a deep burgundy. Red was a good color on him. Without speaking a word, he swept her up in his arms and carted her across the living room to a white painted door. Feeling weightless in his arms—the man must lift some serious pounds at the gym—despite the extra baby fat she'd never bothered trying to lose, mostly because that would require—gasp!—giving up her number one and number two indulgences; chocolate and ice cream, she wrapped one arm around his shoulder. At least her love of all things chocolate and sinful hadn't cut short her life.

An asshole with an attitude, a lost conscience, and a nine millimeter had.

With a mental shove, she pushed those unpleasant thoughts aside for now and reached down with her free hand and twisted the doorknob. Jake kicked the door open like a big, fierce warrior, then stopped dead in his tracks.

"What the hell?" they said in unison.

The walls were painted the dull grey of concrete and black shades covered the windows. But the unusual color choices were not the most startling—or noteworthy—aspect of the room. The odd four-poster bed, constructed out of what looked like spare parts from industrial buildings, wasn't even the most surprising. It was kind of cool.

The other furniture in the room, all black, a strange-looking chair suspended from the ceiling, another thing that looked like a kneeler from her grandma's Catholic church, and a variety of other objects that gave the room a medieval-torture-chamber quality and were the most extraordinary items in the room.

Yet, even though the stuff was spooky, it was also intriguing. Claire could imagine herself bent over the top part of that kneeler, her legs spread wide, her bottom being struck and then caressed until she melted into a puddle of goo . . .

Her nether parts warmed.

"Who or what is this friend of yours?" she asked, sounding breathless despite her lack of exertion. She was being held like an infant, for God's sake. Course, it didn't help that her heart was zipping along at a pace at least ten times normal.

"A freelance photographer." He carried her into the room and set her on the bed. "I never expected him to get into this."

"This what? Torture?" she asked absently as she studied the finer aspects of the bed's construction. It was impressive.

"He'd always been so . . . vanilla."

"Vanilla versus what? Is this chocolate? Because if it is then I've just been introduced to a brand of the stuff I've never even dreamed of."

"Let me ask you this." He turned a serious gaze on her. "Have you ever fantasized about being tied up during sex?"

"Can I plead the fifth? I refuse to answer on the grounds that it might incriminate me."

He sat next to her and wrapped his meaty paw around her hand. My, he was a hulk of a man. All hard angles and thick limbs, more substantial than any man she'd ever dated. In a way, his size was a bit intimidating, in a way arousing. Much like the strange furniture in the room.

"I mean, we barely know each other," she continued, staring down at his hands. She wondered how it would feel to have those long, tapered fingers inside her. "Do we have to talk about such personal things? I mean, I was just hoping for some no-strings sex. No offense. I guess I always just assumed most guys would be happy to get that."

"I can't speak for most guys, but I can tell you that I . . ." he stopped and stared at her for a minute. "That's all you want? One night of no-strings sex?"

"Well, maybe a few nights. Do you think John'll be gone for . . . oh, about a week and a half or so?"

"I'm not sure." He didn't look exactly thrilled. "No strings? Huh," he mumbled. "What am I worried about?" Seeming to have made up his mind, he smiled. "Okay. You want no-strings sex, you got it. For nine days and nine nights."

"Perfect." Yippee! She was getting exactly what she'd hoped for, without having to worry about hurting his feelings in the end. "Before we start, do you happen to know if John has a sweet tooth?"

"No. Why?"

"Well, I've had a craving for Ben & Jerry's for ages." She took another look around the death chamber. "Besides, this room is giving me the heebie-jeebies."

"That's perfect. I'm starving too. And although I have to have sex, like, now, I'd rather have something in my stomach. A guy's gotta have his strength. And you're going to need yours too." He winked. "Let's go raid the refrigerator. Maybe we'll find some fun stuff in there, like whipped cream and chocolate sauce."

"Now you're talking!"

Chapter 5

Like two starved college coeds, they charged the kitchen. Jake went for the deli meat, bread, and cheese, erecting a towering sandwich that disappeared in a few gulps. Claire went straight for the dessert. Bless him, John had a freezer full of her favorite flavors. Oh the joy! There was Chunky Monkey . . . and Cherry Garcia . . . and New York Super Fudge Chunk!

Not sure which one to start with, she pulled out all three containers, searched through the drawers until she found a spoon, and, closing her eyes, grabbed one, flipped off the top, and dug in.

"Oh . . ." she said around luscious chocolatey sweetness. "I've wanted some of this stuff for so long," she said with a sigh.

Jake laughed. "You look like you're about to have an orgasm."

"I am!" She giggled.

"Then don't leave me out of the fun." The bag of chips he was about to attack abandoned on the counter, he grabbed a spoon out of the drawer, sat next to her, and reached for the New York Fudge.

She caught his wrist before a single finger had touched

the carton. "Get your own, buster. There's more in the freezer."

"You mean to tell me you won't share a single bite?"

"Nope."

"What if I do this?" He set down his spoon and stripped off his shirt, revealing a broad, muscular chest and flat, chiseled abdomen, both sprinkled with just enough hair to be yummy.

Well, that was one way to get a girl's attention. She felt herself grinning like a goon as she licked the Cherry Garcia off the bottom of her spoon. "Hmmm . . . I might be convinced if you take off your pants too. New York Fudge is, after all, my second favorite."

"Fair enough." His snug jeans hit the floor in a zip and a snap.

He wore those sexy cotton athletic boxers. Black. Snug. There was a notable bulge front and center. Double yum!

She felt a bit of saliva collecting in the corner of her mouth and swallowed. Then, being a good sport—fair was fair—she handed him the container. "That definitely deserves some fudge."

He accepted it with a mischievous grin that made her hot and cold at the same time. He flipped off the top with two thumbs, then scooped out a large spoonful. His gaze riveted to her, he lifted his spoon, but stopped short of his mouth and smoothed the ice cream on his chest. "Oh dear. I'm such a klutz. But what to do? What to do?" he said, in the most overdramatic voice she'd ever heard. He topped it off with an exaggerated sigh. "I could use a napkin but it would be such a crime to waste all this delicious dessert."

"You bet it would." Knowing he was playing around yet aghast that he'd do something so sacrilegious with her ice cream—okay, okay, she hadn't bought it, but still!—she shrieked and ran to him, spoon in hand, prepared to scrape it off his skin. He caught her wrist before she had a chance to get even a teaspoon of it off. "What're you doing? It's melting."

"I think a tongue might work better," he suggested with a stone-cold straight face that belied the teasing tone of his voice.

Despite her worries about the chocolate and vanilla that were quickly liquefying thanks to the heat radiating from the man's chest, she giggled. What could be better? Chocolate with sex. Sex with chocolate. It was the kind of combination dreams were made of.

Not waiting for a second invitation, she ran her tongue up his torso, starting at his navel and traveling up over tight abs and a toned chest. He smelled like man and leather and tasted even better. After licking every bit of the remaining dessert, she smacked her lips and planted them on one of his tight, pebbled nipples.

He groaned in appreciation, which made her all the hotter.

Encouraged, she dropped one hand to his lap to fondle the bulge in cotton spandex while she sucked and nipped at his other nipple.

Clearly grateful, a deep rumbly growl emanated from him, which seemed to zig and zag through her innards like lightning.

All kinds of parts warmed in response and she grinned, caught the elastic waist of his snug boxers with her thumb, and slipped her fingertips inside.

Oh, heaven was a mere few inches from her grasp.

He caught her wrist before she found her target. "Uh-uh. You've put me through enough misery."

"Well, who's to blame for that? Let me see. Who started it by smearing New York Fudge on his chest? Was it moi? I don't think so."

"Very cute."

"I try." She fluttered her eyelashes and donned her "cute is me" smile.

"Believe me, you succeed."

"Glad to hear it," she said with a satisfied nod. Then, her satisfaction faded a bit as she noted his amused expression. Amused was not the same as hot and horny. "Although on second thought, tonight I should probably shoot for a little more than cute. After all, cute is the word most people use to describe things like babies, or puppies. Not a wanton sex kitten." She purred.

"Mmmm . . ." he said, grinning. The amused expression had taken on a bit of a naughty glint. That was a marked improvement. "I sense an inequality here. I'm down to my socks and shorts and you have all your clothes on."

"These can hardly be called clothes." She lifted the filmy robe away, allowing the light behind her to shine through it. "I've seen shadows that have more substance."

"Still, fair's fair. Off with the nightie . . ." He stood and slowly leaned toward the left. ". . . if you want any more of this!" Before she could stop him, he snatched her Cherry Garcia off the table and held it over his head.

"That is so immature," she said, hopping on tiptoe, trying in vain to reclaim what was rightfully hers. "Stealing someone's dessert and using it as bribery. I feel like I'm back in grade school again."

"Hey, I undressed for a single bite of the fudge stuff. A whole pint ought to cost you something."

"But you didn't . . ." She stopped and admired the way his hands held overhead emphasized the sexy muscles of his shoulders and arms. Some parts bulged, others stretched into tight sinewy lines. It was almost yummier than the ice cream he was holding more than eight feet in the air . . . mighty close to the incandescent overhead light . . . which produced a decent amount of heat, she bet . . . "Okay, okay. You win," she conceded dramatically. Fighting a smile, she untied the small ribbon at her neck and let the robe slide off her shoulders. It landed on the floor in a puddle of pink.

Jake watched with blazes in his eyes. Those flames lit a few inside her body and she shuddered as his heated gaze traveled oh-so-slowly over her form. She felt like he was looking straight through the nightgown. When he licked his lips and said, "Tasty," she figured her initial feeling was accurate.

To double-check, she glanced down.

Well, she could see part of the reason for his reaction. Her nipples were hard little peaks, poking at the thin fabric. She unfastened the tiny buttons at the neck as slowly as she could, figuring the longer she made him wait the better.

"This stuff's melting," he said, urging her to speed up her little striptease.

It worked. She undid the remaining buttons as quickly as she could, then lifted the nightgown up over her head and tossed it on the floor.

He lowered his arm and fumbled with the ice cream container, juggling it between his hands, his eyes wide with appreciation. Thankfully, he caught the cardboard container within inches of it striking the floor and set it on the table. "Here you are. You've definitely earned it." He visibly swallowed, then muttered, "Wow. Why the hell did I wait so long to do this?"

Not so hungry anymore, at least not for food, she replaced the covers on all three quarts and put them back in the freezer. Despite her lust, she saw no need to waste perfectly good ice cream.

She didn't get more than two steps before Jake caught her by the shoulders and drilled her with a piercing stare.

"You are the most beautiful woman I've ever seen."

She briefly considered tossing back a teasing retort about him saying that to all women he saw in their underwear but quickly reconsidered. His expression was so sincere she just couldn't do that to him. Unfortunately, with her natural response stifled, she had nothing else to say.

But that was just fine, as it turned out. He tipped his head and moistened his lips with his tongue.

The tip meant a kiss. Yippee!

She mirrored his actions and closed her eyes, eager to taste him, to feel his hard frame pressed against her soft one, to fill her nostrils with his sweet scent.

Wowzers!

Now, some guys were terrible kissers, all tongue, rooting around in a girl's mouth like a blind mole. Those guys never refined their technique, generally because kissing was nothing more than a short prelude to sex. Guys like her ex-fiancé.

Then there were those few who had somehow learned the true art of kissing, knew how to use soft lips and tongue and teeth to make a woman quiver with delight. Those who kissed to give and receive pleasure and appreciated kissing as more than a means to an end.

Jake Faron was definitely a member of the latter group.

Claire's knees buckled and she threw her arms up, looping them around his neck where she could hang on. Her tongue tangoed with his, stroking, tasting, writhing, much like she expected her entire body to do in a few short moments. She flattened her breasts against his trunk and ground her pelvis into his leg. Okay, maybe she was in writhing mode already. Who wouldn't be after nine years of abstinence and years of mole-kissing before that?

He broke the kiss much too soon for her satisfaction.

"What'd you stop for?" She asked, her arms still wrapped tightly around his neck. "In case you couldn't tell, I was enjoying that. Immensely."

His head dropped for a brief second and she had no doubt he was looking at her skimpily covered nether regions, drenching wet, rubbing like a horny cat against his leg. "Oh, I could tell. But . . ." He gently pried her fingers off his neck and pulled her arms down to her sides. "I didn't get to eat my ice cream yet."

"Who cares about that now? I don't. And I'm a Ben & Jerry's fanatic. Their Web site is—was—my homepage."

He chuckled and poked her nose like a man might do a sassy child. "Not very patient, are we?"

The indignity! She was no whiny kid, thank you very much. "You have no idea how patient I've had to be." The song "Anticipation" buzzed through her head. *An. Tis. Ipa. Tion . . . it's making me wait.*

"It'll be worth it." He reached into the freezer, grabbed a carton, and popped off the lid. Then he dug out a big heaping spoonful, stuffed the container back into the freezer and carried the full spoon toward her with a wicked glimmer in his eye.

"What are you doing?" Out of instinct, she took a few steps backward.

"I'm going to eat my ice cream," he answered flatly, and he stepped even closer.

"Why risk losing it on the floor?" she said to his nipple, since his head was way up there but his nipple was right here, pink and tight and yummy. "Just eat it, for heaven's sake." *And then let's get to the good part.*

"Because I want to do this." With his free hand, he gently pushed on her shoulder, coaxing her to sit. Breathless, her heart beating against her breastbone, she fell back into a chair.

Then he straddled her lap.

Oh boy, this was a position she could appreciate. Eye to navel with a man who looked like a model for a workout rag, his erect rod snug in cotton and only inches away. Thick, smooth-skinned thighs parted, straddling her legs. She imagined how silky his tanned skin would feel under her fingertips, how it would taste. . . .

Like a child let loose in a candy store, she didn't know

where to begin. She gripped one thick thigh in each of her hands. Hard muscle under velvet skin. Nice! What next? Lick stomach? Already done that. Dig into those drawers and see what she found? Now that was a possibility!

Clearing his throat, evidently to capture her wandering attention, he held that spoon over her breasts. She met his hot gaze and smothered a moan. Her lips suddenly dry, she licked them.

With a twist of his wrist and a chuckle, he dumped the spoonful of ice cream on her chest.

"Yikes!" She gasped. It was cold! She didn't jump, but she sure wanted to. The chill eased slightly as the glob slowly slid between her breasts and down to her stomach. Melting, she practically slid out of the chair.

He backed up a step or two, which was a major bummer. Her thighs contracted, eager to close around his thick form. Her hands itched to reach out and stroke his velvet skin. Her nose strained to find his scent. She leaned forward but before she reached him, he shook his head. "Don't move."

She shuddered as his words reverberated through her body.

He lowered his head. His tongue ran down the cleft between her breasts and her stomach muscles instantly clenched. Her breathing quickened and her hands lifted to his arms, her fingertips pressing again firm muscle sheathed in smooth skin. When his tongue traced a slick path up to one nipple she shivered. Goosebumps coated her arms as fevered chills buzzed up her spine. He closed his warm, moist mouth around the nipple, suckling and nipping until it was a tight pebbled peak. She dug her fingernails in deeper and pulled as need pulsed through her body with every gentle suck. Dizzy, perspiring, trembling, she parted her legs wider and ground her pelvis into his legs.

Then he turned his attention to the other breast. She dropped her head back and groaned. Her kitty was feeling mighty neglected, wet and empty and throbbing, though she was genuinely appreciating the thorough attention he was giving each breast. Since on a good day her breasts filled the cups of her AA bra, and her tiny pink nipples were no bigger than nickels, her ex-fiancé had rarely even touched them, let alone given them the kind of gentle loving care this man was lavishing on each one. She could only imagine what else was in store for her!

Anticipation made her even hotter, which made her wish he had some more of that ice cream to spread over her chest. Cool and creamy on her hot skin, it was like a soothing balm.

Not sure what to do with her hands, she lifted them to tangle her fingers in the curls at his nape. His hair was silky, not wiry like curly hair could be, and it smelled like suntan lotion. She didn't have the willpower to move her hands from the soft thickness. Her fingers massaging his scalp, her hips rocking back and forth, back and forth, her breasts being kneaded, sucked, and nipped, she let a low groan of pleasure slip through her lips.

"You like?" he whispered, grazing her nipple with his teeth.

Her eyes slid shut as she breathed the words, "You bet." She shuddered as waves of longing pooled between her legs. "Oh God. No one's done this before."

"Kissed your breasts?" He nuzzled the sensitive skin that felt like it was on fire.

"Not like you are doing," she whispered through gritted teeth.

"That's a shame. I'll try to make up for it, then." He expelled a warm rush of air against her skin, making her fingers tighten into a fist at his nape.

"That's okay. You don't need to right now." She tilted

her hips and, catching his wrist, dragged his flattened palm down her belly. "I'm kinda anxious to get to the next step," she confessed.

"Is that so?" His chuckle rumbled low in her belly. It almost felt better than what he was doing to her chest. Almost.

"My panties are sopping wet," she whispered on a sigh.

"Really?" He kneeled between her legs and kissed her stomach. Her muscles tightened under his mouth, and her breath hitched in her chest.

"I'm sure you've felt it by now. I've been rubbing against you like a cat in heat."

He trailed kisses lower, to the waistband of her panties, then repositioned himself at her feet, pressed her knees together and hooked his thumbs in the waistband of her panties and pulled.

All for what was about to happen, she opened her eyes and lifted her bottom off the chair.

Off came the panties. Yay! Now, all she needed to do was get his off. She shifted forward, reaching for his shorts, but he caught her wrists.

He shook his head. "Uh-uh. Not yet."

What the heck was he waiting for? A written invitation?

Chapter 6

"Ohhh. I get it. You have a . . . a quick trigger?" Claire asked when he didn't explain why he was putting her off, again. That was the only explanation that made any sense whatsoever.

"No, I just like to be in control in the bedroom."

"We're in the kitchen. That's my turf," she reasoned, not exactly too hellbent on taking control. If she were honest with herself, she'd admit nothing turned her on more than a man who would take control during sex. The idea sent shudders of excitement down to her toes and back up again.

He rested his hands on her knees and looked into her eyes. "You're trembling. Are you scared?"

"Heck no," she answered between panting breaths and quivers. "Just extremely horny."

"Okay. But promise me you'll tell me if I do anything you don't like."

"I promise. But I don't see that happening. We haven't gotten to the good stuff yet and you're already ranked the best screw of my life."

"Well, that's saying something, I suppose," he said with a smile.

Finally having caught her breath, she said, "If there's

one complaint I have it's that you're taking too darn long to get to the good part."

"That's your mistake," he said on a chuckle. "Every part is the good part. Not just the intercourse."

"Is that right? Then I've been wrong all these years. Huh," she joked as she tried to sneak her hands lower. That bulge in his drawers was looking too yummy to not give it a try.

Naturally, he saw her coming from a mile away and gently brushed her hands away. "Uh-uh!"

"This is not fair." She faked a pout as she crossed her arms over her chest.

"You won't be complaining in a minute." With his hands on her knees, he gently urged them apart. Then he lowered his head.

He wasn't . . .

Oh, God! He was!

He parted her outer lips with his fingers, then gave her sodden sex a shy swipe with his tongue.

She melted.

He moaned.

He did it a second time and, both hot and cold at the same time, she shivered. Her legs trembled, her heart thumped loudly in her ear.

He found her sensitive nub and teased it with thrusts of his tongue and she arched her back, pressing her pelvis up into the air. Her stomach muscles strained, making her breathing ragged once again.

"Oh. My . . ." she murmured.

His mouth doing things she never thought possible to her most sensitive parts, he pushed a finger inside her passage and she just about screamed in relief. To finally have something inside. Oh, it was heaven! He matched the rhythm of his finger thrusts with the rhythm of his tongue and she felt herself soaring toward a powerful climax.

Her eyes closed, she lost touch with the world outside,

experiencing only the sensations he stirred in her body. She could hear herself breathe but not feel it. She could smell the musky scent of her own arousal. Could feel the heat spreading up and out across her chest.

Now this was more like it!

"Are you going to come?" he asked, sounding as breathless as she was.

"Yes. Oh, yes!"

He pulled his finger out just before her sex spasmed and she lifted her head and forced her eyes open. "Hey! What'd you do that for? I was just about ready to . . . you know."

"I've just tasted your most intimate places and you can't say the word 'come'?"

Dizzy and confused and barely able to think, she shrugged and tried to draw her knees closed. "I guess I'm a little funny that way."

"Well, I'm not ready to let you come yet," he said, emphasizing the *c*-word while holding her legs apart.

Well, what does one say to a statement like that? "Okay"? "What d'ya mean I can't come?" "How come I can't come?" None of those options worked for her so she just dropped her head back and waited.

Damn controlling bastard . . . she loved it!

"How about we find a more comfortable place to make love?"

"Oh yeah. The tile's gotta be a killer on the knees." She felt herself cringing.

"Actually, I was thinking more of your back."

"My back is fine . . ." she said, not quite finishing when she caught the mischievous glint in his eye. "Oh." Her cheeks burned.

Standing, he took her hand and led her toward the bedroom, but she didn't eagerly follow him. The dungeon was interesting, but it wasn't exactly romantic. At the moment, she was in the mood for romance.

"Nothing against your pal—or you, for that matter, if you're into that sort of thing—but do we have to go in there?" She pointed at the bedroom door. "I don't think I'm ready for that . . . whatever it is . . . er, yet."

"Fair enough. Is the couch okay?"

"Perfect."

With a slight shift in direction, he led her into the living room. The couch was very long with simple, straight lines. It almost looked like the couch her mom and dad had in their family room back in the seventies, but updated a smidge. It too was a grey. Charcoal. And assuming it might very well be the latest and greatest in living room furnishings, it probably cost a bloody fortune.

"On second thought," she said, standing in front of it. "Maybe we shouldn't . . . I'd hate to leave any stains," she whispered, as if someone else might overhear. She glanced down at the shaggy carpet—another throwback to the seventies. "This carpet looks mighty comfy."

"Works for me. Hang on just a sec." He dashed into the bedroom and returned with some pillows and a blanket. He spread the blanket on the floor, tossed the pillows on top of it, then sat, coaxing her with a jaunty smile to sit next to him. "Come on, love bug. Let's get busy."

"Love bug?" She sat. "Is that supposed to be—" Oh . . .

He didn't even let her finish her sentence, but instead kissed her to heaven and back. He either grew a half-dozen hands all of a sudden or the two he had were very busy. Stroking, exploring, pinching, tickling. Man, did he know how to use those hands.

And that mouth too! She could kiss him forever and ever. Oh . . . and ever! Now flat on her back, she lifted her right hand and tangled her fingers in his silky curls. She explored other parts—parts much farther south—with her left.

He paused long enough to smile and growl some incoherent comment at her. Then he tugged off his snug boxers, revealing his thick, hard penis.

Oh mama! She knew it was big before. But she didn't know how big. Her sex clenched in a spasm.

"Do you like being on bottom or top?" he asked, getting into position on top of her. Clearly he wasn't really interested in her answer. She briefly considered saying top just to see if he would change positions but changed her mind. Truth be told, being on bottom was the best.

"Bottom."

He nudged her knees apart, settled his pelvis between her thighs, and leaning forward, his upper body held off her chest with his bent arms, scooped her head into his palms. His tongue darted out and moistened his lips. "I've been wanting . . . I mean . . . I've waited . . . oh, damn." In a single thrust he buried his rod deep inside her.

She arched her back to take him as deep as possible. "Oh, yes!"

He withdrew and thrust over and over, and she met each thrust with a tip of her pelvis. His groin rubbed her pelvis, creating delicious friction.

The heat pulsing through her body stole her breath. She gasped and tipped her head slightly as Jake nuzzled her neck, his tongue and teeth tickling and making her shiver and sweat at the same time. Goosebumps blanketed one side of her body.

He shifted back a bit, changing angles and holding his body up and away from hers. She wanted to pull him closer again but when she reached for him, he shook his head. "I want to see you."

That was so sweet! Then again, it was also kind of embarrassing. No one had seen her come before. Not even Matt. What if she made a funny face or something?

He balanced himself with one arm and used his free hand to tease her folds and nub and she felt a powerful climax coiling deep in her belly, winding up and out, slowly, slowly.

Who the hell cared what she looked like? She gripped the blanket in her fists, clenched every muscle in her body and let herself go, soaring on wave after wave of mind-blowing, blazing orgasm. She heard his rhythmic grunts as he thrust faster and faster, finding his own release and shooting his seed deep inside her. Her pulsing folds took it all in, milking each drop until they were both trembling, sweaty and satisfied.

Still panting heavily, he pulled out, rolled onto his side and gathered her into his arms. She rested her head on his slick chest, closed her eyes and listened to the quick thrump-bump, thrump-bump of his heart.

She could just imagine what her heart was doing. "Holy smokes!" she said between rapid breaths.

"You . . . you-know-what, didn't you?" He cleared his throat. "I mean, I think I could tell, but I want to make sure."

"Oh yeah. Did I ever. Whew!" She slid the back of her hand across her sweaty forehead.

"Good."

She lay there another few minutes, enjoying the closeness, the scents of man and sex, the sound of his slowing, steady breathing. Her mind wandered, recalling his words as they'd made love. He'd started to say something about waiting. What was that all about?

"Can I ask you a question?" she said, finally, unable to fight her curiosity for another moment.

"Sure." He was stroking her arm gently. Up and down, up and down. It was the sweetest thing. She wondered if he even realized he was doing it.

"When we were . . . er, making love, you said you'd been waiting a long time . . . or something like that. What did you mean? Were you talking about today? Because you sure as heck made me wait way too long. I mean, I'm all for foreplay but that was ridiculous."

"Oh. Yeah. Uh. Exactly. It was killing me too. But wasn't the result worth it?"

"I guess . . ." she said, not quite convinced he was telling her the whole truth. There was something in his voice. "I just thought maybe you meant something else."

"Nope. That was it. I'd been waiting all night," he said a little too eagerly for her to buy.

Huh. Maybe it wasn't fair to wonder what he'd meant, and maybe she didn't deserve to go there—after all, at best she'd be around only a little more than a week—but she ached to know what he'd meant. Right down to her toes.

Maybe tomorrow. Exhausted, she closed her eyes and let his soft, buzzing snore lull her to sleep.

Tomorrow was another day. She'd have more sex. More chocolate. Then do her good deed. Then, at midnight, she'd finally see Matt, find out how he's doing, let him know he didn't have to grieve for her anymore, and hopefully get some answers to some burning questions. By now, he had to have heard who'd killed her. He had to have some information.

Chapter 7

A salad bowl of Cocoa Puffs in front of her, and with a healthy dose of curiosity Claire eyeballed the sleek black computer sitting in the living room. A window into the unknown, it beckoned her with a mightier voice than the chocolatey goodness in front of her. She'd been gone from the earth for nine years. Yeah, it wasn't ninety years . . . or nine hundred . . . and things still looked pretty much the same. The cars still rolled on the ground instead of hovering above it and people still walked on sidewalks rather than zooming through the air with the aid of jet-powered boots, but still, she was curious. What had she missed? Had doctors found a cure for AIDS yet? Or cancer? Had the U.S. come to its senses and elected a woman for president?

Jake was in the shower. She had a few minutes. She crammed her mouth full of crispy chocolate corn, then plopped herself in front of the machine and turned it on.

Whew! That thing hummed right along compared to the computer she'd used at work just before she'd died. It played music and displayed flashing, clear images. It was actually fun clicking between screens! That was a minor miracle in itself. Now, to sign onto the Internet. . . .

Where's the AOL icon?

She couldn't find any kind of sign-on screen, so she just clicked the pretty blue *e* at the bottom. It opened a Yahoo! page, just like that! Wow, another miracle. Instant on, no dialing? No waiting? What a world this was! So far, she was impressed.

She went to her favorite news site, CNN. They had a year-in-review page. That would be a quick and easy way to find out what she'd missed.

She typed in "1996." Nothing too exciting—a few uprisings, Clinton reelected. *Braveheart* released on VHS. Oh! She'd wanted to see that movie! She wondered if there was a movie store close by. They still had those, she hoped.

She tried 1997. What was this? Princess Diana was dead? Well, that was a shocker! And some scientist in Scotland cloned a sheep? Ewww . . . that was just plain weird.

She typed in "1998" and read the headlines. Blah, blah, blah. Military skirmishes, political uprisings and rebellions. Oh, this one's interesting. "A Presidency Mired in Scandal." What kind of trouble did old Billy Boy get himself into now? Did she really care? Nah.

Next, she typed "1999." Nothing too exciting. Next was 2000. Did the whole world shut down like those freaky pseudomilitary groups had claimed it would? She read on. Not a single mention of worldwide disaster. *Ha ha! Stupid gas-mask-hoarding weirdos, you were wrong.*

She heard the water shut off and hurriedly typed "2001." What the hell was this? A plot from a sci-fi movie? New York City was bombed? The Twin Towers were no more? Nuh-uh!

"What're you doing?" Jake asked behind her.

Startled, she practically fell out of the chair. "Oh, shoot! You scared me."

He caught her shoulders. "Sorry. I didn't mean to. What're you reading?"

"Someone's idea of a sick joke, that's what." She punched the power button on the monitor, shutting off the image of the blazing towers. "I didn't expect something like that on CNN's site, for God's sake."

"What?" He reached around her to turn the monitor back on but she caught his wrist.

"Please don't. That picture gave me the willies. It was creepier than that torture chamber in there," she said, motioning toward the bedroom. "I feel sick."

"Then you'd better come away from here. Let me help." With warm, gentle hands he helped her stand and steered her back toward the comfort of Cocoa Puffs. She sat at the table and stared into her bowl, but instead of milk and brown corn puffs all she saw was that awful picture in her head. The Twin Towers in flames.

It had to be a photograph from a movie or something. Yeah, that was it. A picture from a movie. Probably directed by Steven Spielberg. He was a master at illusion. *Jurassic Park* had given her nightmares for weeks.

A little more settled now that she was sure she'd figured that terrible image was not real, she polished off her cereal, then put her dishes into the dishwasher. Jake drank a shake of some kind. It looked yummy but based on his grimace she doubted it tasted as good as it looked.

Her appetite finally sated—she couldn't remember the last time she'd been so starving—she hopped into the shower. The hot water felt wonderful and she probably stood in there a good forty-five minutes, long enough for Jake to get worried and come knocking on the door to check on her. She took his concerned, "Are you okay in there or do I need to call for help?" as a cue to shut off the water.

She wrapped herself in a thick towel the size of a small quilt and barefooted it to the bedroom to search for something to wear. John wouldn't happen to keep a few pieces of women's clothing around, would he? She pulled open the closet to check. The minute she had the doors opened, she slammed them shut.

That was no clothes closet. It was a . . . a weapon closet. Full of whips and chains and various torture devices. Blech!

Still, even though the sight of those things had given her a serious case of the icks, she couldn't help sneaking another peek. Morbid curiosity. There were several kinds of whips, some made of leather, some of latex—or so she assumed. Some had long narrow poles with soft tickly ends. She ran her fingers through the three-inch-long fringe. Oh. That felt nice. *I wonder what it would feel like on my backside. . . .*

Her face and chest warmed. Time to get out of there. Now!

She slammed the door shut and went to another set of doors on the opposite wall. Finally, clothing! All men's, unfortunately. But she wasn't surprised.

"Are you doing okay in there?" Jake called through the closed bedroom door.

"Yep. Fine. Just . . . er, looking for something to wear. I was hoping your friend John had a lady friend who made a habit of leaving her clothes behind." She pulled out a pair of slacks and held them up to herself. Good grief! The darn things were so long the waist came up to her armpits and at least three inches of leg still dragged on the floor.

John was a giant. A giant with a torture chamber, who wore a lot of black, she noted as she rummaged through his clothes in the hope of finding something—anything—she could wear.

"In case you haven't noticed, my buddy's a little tall," Jake said through the door.

"It's hard not to notice." Giving up on the closet, she went to the chest of drawers.

Bingo! A pair of enormous gray sweatpants would do the trick. At least they wouldn't drag on the floor, thanks to the elastic at the ankles. And a matching sweatshirt would keep her warm. It wasn't exactly stylish but beggars couldn't be choosers. Of course her only footwear, the feathered pink mules, would look a little silly. Maybe later she'd do some shopping . . . if she could find out how to get some money.

Yeah, that was it. High heels, sweatpants that needed suspenders to keep them up, and a sweatshirt that skimmed the tops of her knees. This was a fashion disaster! It was time to give Bonnie a call.

Dressed, she did her best to fix her hair, then went out into the living room to locate her shoes, wherever they'd landed. She couldn't even remember having taken them off.

With a friendly smile that made her feel all warm and toasty on the inside, Jake met her in the hallway. It was a crying shame this couldn't be a longer-term arrangement. She was really enjoying his company, already.

"You look fantastic," he said in a low, sexy voice that promised a lot more of what last night had brought.

"In these old rags? You're being kind," she teased.

"Sweetheart, you're so gorgeous you'd make potato sacks look good."

She giggled. "Flattery will get you everywhere."

"I'm counting on it," he said with a wink.

Her cheeks warmed. "I bet you are. But first things first. I have a phone call to make and an errand to run. Oh, and by the way, your very large friend won't get angry at me for borrowing a few of his clothes, will he? Gauging from the size of this stuff, I'm guessing he's not the kind of person I'd want to piss off."

"I can't remember the last time I saw him wearing those sweats. He probably won't even realize they're gone. You look mighty cute in them." He blocked her entry into the living room with his broad-shouldered, hunky body, so she had no choice but to charm her way past him.

What a shame.

She grinned and sighed. "Here we go with the cute thing again. Last I checked I didn't resemble a puppy or a baby. Couldn't you pick a more appropriate adjective? Something like—urg!"

He interrupted her mindless babbling with a kiss that nearly knocked her off her feet. Whatever she had started to say dropped instantly from her mind as she kissed him back. He was still wearing only a towel, which was mighty convenient at the moment.

Easy access.

He didn't even complain when she ripped it off and tossed it across the room. And it seems he had no issues with the cool air either. His erection rose to full staff within a heartbeat.

It didn't take much longer for him to remove her baggy sweatshirt and pants. Because she had no underwear, she was naked to his touch in a snap. And he took full advantage. Every inch of her skin was explored as his mouth continued to work magic with hers. Her neck, breasts, stomach, armpits—good thing she'd shaved every part of her the day of her death—were stroked, touched, and tickled.

Yes, she was well on her way to making up for nine years of abstinence in the space of twelve hours. The man was a sexual dynamo!

A part of her still marveled that he was there, with her, giving her the most toe-curling kisses and shiver-producing strokes of her life. What had she done to deserve this? And why hadn't some lucky woman grabbed this sweet hunk of man meat, hauled him to the altar, and made him her own?

He scooped her into his arms and carted her across the room. Content with focusing on sounds, scents, and touches, she closed her eyes and held on, kissing and nipping whatever skin came into contact with her mouth. Seconds later she felt him set her down on something soft and climb on top of her.

Unlike last night, this time he seemed to lack control.

There was no drawn-out foreplay. After a few intimate strokes, which she knew weren't necessary—she was blazing hot just from his kisses—he thrust inside her.

Her mouth had been busy somewhere near his nipple when he'd plunged inside but it wasn't so busy she couldn't let out a little moan of gratitude. In return, he gave her the pleasure of several slow, deep thrusts before switching to a faster pace. Like magic, his penis found every sensitive spot inside her and stroked, stroked, stroked until she was trembling, slick and sweaty and writhing under Jake like a victim of a life-threatening fever.

Which she was.

The fever burning inside her was threatening to steal her breath. The sound of her labored breathing huffed in her ears as she clung to Jake's sweat-slicked shoulders and tipped her pelvis to meet his thrusts. Coiling deep inside, building in strength like a summer storm, a powerful orgasm drew closer until it was there, quaking her, hurtling her up to the heavens and beyond. She heard him as he found his release too. The instant of extra fullness sent her back to the stars in a second orgasm. Two orgasms! She'd never come twice before. Forget the sexual dynamo, the man was a master.

Slowly, like a feather dropped from a third-storey window, she drifted back to earth. When she landed, she sighed, wrapped her arms around his wide torso, and squeezed.

Heavy, lying sprawled on top of her, he didn't respond.

While she knew that after sex men tended to look like a possum discovered by a hound dog, she'd occasionally worried that one day she'd actually kill a man during sex. It wasn't unheard of. Sex was a physically demanding activity, taxing muscles, heart, lungs.

She poked Jake in the ribs. "Hey, tell me you're still alive or I'm going to scream."

"Don't scream. I'm okay." He pulled his softening erection out, then rolled heavily to the side. Suddenly feeling light she drew in a much-needed deep breath and blinked open her eyes.

She screamed. Not a long, blood-curdling, heroine-in-a-slasher-movie kind of scream, but a short, shrill, "Yikes!"

"What? What?" Jake sat bolt upright. Clearly bewildered, he looked around. "I'm alive . . . I think." He explored his face with his big hands. "Everything feels okay."

"How did we end up in here?" she asked, ignoring his momentary confusion regarding his status as a living being for the present.

There were some things more important, like the fact that they were lying in the middle of that freakish-looking bed in that icky torture chamber room.

"You don't remember? I carried you in here."

"I don't. I guess I . . . er . . ." she felt her cheeks flaming. "I was distracted a little."

"I'm sorry it took you by surprise." He stroked her cheek gently. "You'll forgive me, won't you?"

"Yes. In time," she added, even though she'd already forgiven him. Who could stay mad at a man who was so sweet and attentive? "Next time, warn me if you take me into the deepest depths of the dungeon, would ya?"

"Fair enough." He chuckled and she marveled at what an utterly charming sound it was. "Honestly, you're not that creeped out by this room, are you?"

"Honestly?" She bit back the answer that wanted to slip through her lips—hell yes!—and instead took a moment to formulate a more thought-out answer. "Yes and no." How was that for mixed messages?

"Hmmm. That's a little vague. Care to clarify? Not that you have to. Since we'll only be together a few days. But I'd . . . I'd like to know."

Well, that part about being together a few days really put a damper on her mood. Now she was not only creeped-out but also bummed too. Did he have to remind her of that little bit of news? With her body still twitching from their lovemaking? And the scent of him all over her skin?

Still, she craved to be close to him. To tell him her deepest secrets, to explore her darkest fantasies. "I've never been tied up, not even with a silk scarf. But all my life, ever since I read some stupid seventies romance novel my mother'd left lying around, I've fantasized about it." She squirmed a little, embarrassed by what she was admitting. Aloud! She'd never talked about sex to anyone, not even a shrink. Or her fiancé. "I've always wondered what it would feel like having a strong man I trust take control and throw me over his lap to spank me, to relinquish control, be bound, my legs . . ." She touched her red-hot face. "I can't. This is too embarrassing. I feel like I'm having phone sex. Maybe I should add a few moans for effect."

He smiled into her eyes. Not the kind of smile a guy gives a girl when he'd rather be throwing on his clothes and running for the front door. That was a relief! No, his gaze was fixed to hers and his smile was warm and sweet and encouraging.

She felt her breathing slow, which made her realize she'd been breathing fast.

"Thank you for sharing that with me."

"So, now that I admitted the lamest—"

"It wasn't lame," he interrupted.

"Okay. Most embarrassing thing ever. How about you doing a little confessing too? Fair's fair."

"Okay." He bit his lip as he thought, which made her want to taste him all over again, even though the sweet flavor of his kisses still lingered in her mouth. "I've always wanted to spank a woman."

She slapped his shoulder. "You're making fun of me!"

"No, I swear it. I'd never make fun of you. I'm telling the truth. Actually, if you want to know the whole truth, I've spanked a woman before and I liked it. A lot. I've even tried all this stuff before." He motioned toward the assorted objects-d'kink scattered around the room.

Well, that answered a few questions. But one particular question popped into her head and she had to ask, "So is there really a John or is this your place and you were too embarrassed to admit it?"

"I can see why you'd think that, but no, I didn't lie. John's a freelance photographer, a very talented one, I'll add. He's had stuff published in all the national papers, even a few magazines. He's never here so I figured it would be a good place to hang out for a few days. But take my word for it, I was as surprised as you were when I stepped into this room. I . . . haven't been here in a while. The last time I was, it was your typical bachelor's bedroom, white, a king-sized Serta lying on the bare wood floor and an ugly dresser missing half the knobs. This stuff is all new."

"Lucky me," she said under her breath.

"Huh?"

"Uh . . ." she coughed. "I had a frog in my throat. Okay." She got up and started wandering around looking for her discarded clothes. Jake had a good arm. Should've been a quarterback. None of the pieces were close by. Her shirt was lying in a heap in one corner, her pants way across the room, dangling from a lampshade. "So, John's a photographer with a kinky side. What about you? You never told me what you do for a living. I've been curious for ages, ever since I saw that tank you drive."

"I'm a . . . physician."

"Oh! Well, that explains your hands." She stepped into the sweatpants and pulled them up to just below her breasts.

"My . . . hands?"

"Yeah." She pulled the sweatshirt on, then poked both arms into the sleeves. "They're strong and gentle at the same time. I should've known. Then again, I've never dated a doctor before." Ack! Had she just implied they were dating? "What kind of doctor are you?" she hurriedly added, hoping he didn't notice her blunder. "No, wait. Let me guess." She rounded the bed, then sat on the edge next to him and studied his face, like he was going to give her a hint somehow. She got nothing, no doctor vibe. "Mmmm . . . Pediatrician."

"Nope."

"General Practice?"

"Nope."

"Ob-Gyn?"

"Nope."

"Thank God!" she blurted before she could stop herself. There was something downright icky about dating a guy who spent all day long between strange women's legs.

He laughed. "Give up yet?"

"Yes."

"I'm a pediatric neurologist."

"Impressive," she said with a nod. "What with all the kids you must be able to . . . cure? Uh . . . what does a pediatric neurologist treat? I've never visited a pediatric neurologist."

"That's a good thing. My patients have a variety of neurological disorders, seizures, learning disabilities—those kinds of things, in layman's terms. I rarely 'cure' my patients. Most of the time their conditions are irreversible but I help them and their families the best I can."

"Ugh. Sounds kind of depressing."

"Believe it or not, it wasn't."

She smiled because she didn't know what else to do, and because she just felt like smiling. It was easy to smile when she was with this man. He was a whole lot deeper than she'd ever imagined he would be. *Goes to show, you can't judge a guy by the color of his leather.*

He glanced at the clock. "This day is slipping away from us. Maybe we'd better get going."

"Good idea." She scrambled to her feet, even though

she'd like nothing better than to curl up in that freakish bed with Jake and listen to him talk all afternoon. Unfortunately, things being what they were, she had to get hustling. Obviously, she wasn't going to be able to do her good act for him, so she had precious little time to find a person in need of a little kindness.

A little bit of money and some less ghoulish clothing might help. If she were to approach someone on the street in this getup they'd probably scream in terror, she told herself as she plucked the card out of her pink mules, then slid them on her feet. *Hello? Can you say "Tacky"?*

"Do you think John would mind if I made a long-distance phone call?" she asked, staring down at her feet. Even a pair of ten-dollar Keds would be an improvement. But she wouldn't make the call without permission. Dialing purgatory had to be a toll charge at least, maybe even international billing. It could cost John a serious chunk of change.

"I'm sure he won't mind."

"Great!" She eyeballed the phone sitting on the desk next to the front door and ran across the room to grab it before she chickened out. Then she dialed Bonnie's number and waited.

It rang once, twice, three times. Then click.

"Hello, this is Bonnie . . ."

"Bonnie!" Claire said in a hushed voice. "This is Claire. I'm not having a life or death—"

". . . I can't come to the phone right now but if you leave a message I'll be sure to call you back as soon as possible."

Voicemail? Her caseworker had voicemail? Ugh!

She slammed down the phone and turned. *Now what? Think, think, think*. Shoot! What good was a caseworker if you couldn't get a hold of her when you needed her? Claire needed money. Period. How anyone could expect her to accomplish anything flat broke and running around the world in her pj's was beyond her. They were asking for a miracle!

Time to suck it up and ask Jake for some cash. Certainly he would understand and, being a doctor and all, he couldn't be too strapped for cash, could he?

God, she hated asking people for money! Especially the guy she was sleeping with for a few days—using like a big hunk of sexy meat—and then running out on. But if she didn't get out there in that big world and do something nice for someone soon, she'd be back up in purgatory waiting for ten years to pass. Who knew where Jake would be by then. A smart, adorable, sexy doctor, for God's sake! He'd surely be claimed by some woman by then.

Some lucky bitch. She gave herself a mental slap. She had no right to be jealous! He was a free agent, couldn't be expected to wait to spend a week and a half with her every ten years. *But maybe if I made it extra good for him? Shut up, selfish! Nothing like having an argument with yourself to put you in the mood to do some charity.*

She gave him a doleful I'm-sorry-for-asking-you-this smile. "I don't suppose I could borrow a few dollars from you? Just until I can get to the bank."

He gave her the same smile right back. "I'm sorry, but . . ." He spun around. "Wait a minute. John usually keeps a stash hidden away just in case he gets a late night craving for McDonald's." In three long strides he was across the room, rummaging through the contents of a floor-to-ceiling bookshelf. "He used to keep it in a cigar box on the bottom shelf of his old bookshelf but now he's got all new furniture. Who knows where it might be."

She watched him search in a frenzy that seemed much too enthusiastic for a man who should be rolling in dough. *Must have to spend a bloody fortune for malpractice insurance. I've heard about that. Either that or the gas he must have to feed that Hummer. That thing has to suck up gas like an elephant in a watering hole.* "Do you want some help?"

"Sure."

She began rummaging around in drawers until she hit pay dirt—if you could call a couple fives and a roll of quarters a fortune—in the sofa table drawer. "Here we are."

"What'd you find?"

"About twenty dollars. Do you need some too?"

"How about we split it sixty-forty? You get more?"

"Fair enough. Uh . . . how much would that be? Would eight bucks be good?" She busted open the quarter roll and counted out two dollars to add to the two fives and gave the rest to him.

"Plenty. Thanks."

They looked at each other and after a brief tense moment started laughing.

"How pathetic we are," she said between guffaws.

"You'd think we were a couple of kids rummaging around in our mother's purse for spare change," he said.

They laughed some more and then ran to the front door.

"Gotta go," she said as she pulled open the door.

"Me too," he said as he motioned for her to go first. "Meet you back here in a couple of hours?"

"Sure."

"I'll leave the door unlocked." He pulled it shut as he stepped out into the cramped landing at the top of the stairs.

"Are you sure it's safe? I mean, John has some pretty nice stuff in there. I'd hate to see anything happen to it."

"Yeah. This neighborhood is safe. Besides, we'll only be gone a couple of hours."

I hope even less than that. Standing so close she could identify what brand of deodorant he used—Brut. She tipped her head back to look up at his face. It was a long way up, especially when a girl was standing nipple to belly—her nipples to his belly—with the man of her dreams.

She sighed as she was lost in the deepest, darkest blue eyes she'd ever seen. They were the color of grape juice. Purple blue.

"Better go." He didn't move toward the stairs and neither did she.

"Yeah."

They both stood there, frozen, like a couple of horny teenagers about to say goodnight.

Finally, he broke the spell by looking up. "See you in a couple of hours."

"You can count on it."

"We can have some lunch and then dessert." He winked and she shuddered.

Oh yeah, dessert was sounding great. In fact, she might be convinced to have dessert before lunch. . . .

He skipped down the stairs, much lighter on his feet than she would've expected, considering his size, then at the bottom held the door open for her. She followed, not nearly as lithe or coordinated as he. She sort of stumbled and tripped her way down, thanks to her slippy-soled, flippy-floppy mules, like an elephant on stilettos, then missed the last step entirely and fell into his arms.

Okay, so she did that last part on purpose. She couldn't help herself. He was standing there looking so yummy and strong.

After copping a feel or two she forced herself to stand on her own. She gave him one last smile, a sexy one, just in case he had any thoughts of pulling a disappearing act on her, and then walked down the street in search of the first person who needed some help.

She hoped she wouldn't have to go far. And just in case, she stopped at the dumpy shoe store at the corner and bought herself last year's rejection on clearance—a hideous pink and black model with flashy zigs and zags on the sides and two-toned shoelaces.

Her mules wrapped snugly in the plastic bag, a little over a dollar left in her pocket, she headed back out to look for her charity-case-in-waiting.

Chapter 8

Two hours later Claire was walking a whole lot more slowly, thanks to the blisters burning the backs of her ankles. Damned cheap shoes! Frustration also slowed her progress. Where was a granny who needed someone to carry her packages when you needed one? Or even a dog that had leaped over a fence.

Darn it! The closest she'd come was helping a little girl Claire thought had lost her mommy. Unfortunately, that was no little girl. To Claire's defense, she'd never seen a . . . what name did short-statured people formerly known as midgets go by these days, anyway? The woman in question ended up being a thirty-five-year-old waitress on her lunch break. The lit cigarette should've been a clue. Then again, Claire thought maybe ten-year-olds were smoking these days.

Her stomach grumbled, reminding her of Jake, his promise of lunch . . . and dessert . . . and she briefly considered going back to the apartment, partaking, and then heading out again, but she quickly pushed that notion aside. She had a feeling procrastination had played a big role in her landing in purgatory in the first place and she wasn't about to take the chance that it could get her sent back before she was ready to go.

No. Like it or not, she'd have to stay out there, wearing those awful-fitting clothes and butt-ugly shoes until she found someone to help.

Maybe she could give Bonnie another call? Ask for some money. Then she could head to the first Goodwill, make a donation and be done with it.

She supposed that would be too easy but it was worth a shot. She tried the first payphone she found. It was deader than she was the day before yesterday but just for kicks she punched Bonnie's number anyway.

It rang! Joy of joys! She just might get through.

Ring . . . ring . . . ring . . .

"Hello, this is Bonnie . . ."

"Darn it." She got the stupid voicemail again. Claire started to hang up.

But as her hand arced through the air, she heard a small voice say, "Hello? Hello? Who's there?"

She clapped the phone to her ear. "Bonnie? Is that you? Oh my gosh, I can't believe I finally got you. I need some help and—"

"Excuse me, but who's calling?"

"Good grief! How could I forget to tell you that much? You probably have a huge caseload and since I'm calling from a pay phone, the caller ID—do you have that up there?—it probably wouldn't tell you who's calling. Name's Claire. Claire Weiss. You told me to call if I was in trouble."

"Hi, Claire. I remember you. I like your mules, by the way. My favorite color's pink." She sighed, sounding like a child staring at the Toys-R-Us Christmas catalog. "I just wish my mom had put my favorite pink dress on me the day I . . . er, how can I help you, Claire?"

"Well, this isn't a life-or-death situation or anything but I was wondering how I'd go about getting some money."

"Money? For what?"

"For . . ." She considered lying but for some reason she suspected Bonnie would somehow know she was lying, even if she wasn't able to recognize Claire by her voice, and clearly couldn't read her mind. Besides, fibbing to a representative of His Most Holy probably wasn't the best idea. ". . . money for me to buy something so I can do my good deed," she confessed.

"You don't need money for that," Bonnie said in a scolding voice. There was something very wrong about being reprimanded by a toddler with duckies on her dress and a baby dolly; still, Claire held her tongue. "Besides, I'm already in big trouble because I bent the rules. You read the contract, remember? I can't give you anything until you've done something good. So go do something good already."

"No," Claire corrected. "I *tried* to read the contract. The pages were blank. So how could I remember what they said?" She shifted her weight and waited for Bonnie to tell her some good news, like she'd bend the rules again and give her what she wanted. When Bonnie didn't tell her what she'd hoped, Claire asked, "You bent the rules? For me? How?"

"That apartment you've been . . . having so much fun in," Bonnie said with a cough that suggested she knew exactly what Claire and Jake had been doing inside it. That little revelation made Claire mighty uncomfortable. Who would've thought she'd be spied upon? During her most private moments? By a kid just out of diapers? "There was supposed to be someone inhabiting it this week," Bonnie continued. "I had to make some things happen so it would be empty for you."

"Well, gosh! Some things? I hope no one was hurt on my account."

"Nope. It was nothing that bad. But it was still against the rules and you have no idea what kind of trouble I'm in now. So don't ask me to break any more rules for you. Because I can't. So there. Bye."

Click.

Claire stared at the phone, then placed it back on its cradle. Well, that was an eye-opener! So much for divine intervention . . . and privacy. To think that innocent child was watching as they . . . Eew!

Fighting a case of the heebie-jeebies, she walked down the street, heading back in the general direction of Jake and their love nest. Her mind was not on where she was going as she walked, but instead scrambling to come up with an idea for a good deed that did not involve the exchange of currency.

When she concentrated that hard, she saw, heard, or sensed very little around her, something that had driven her mother nuts when she was a kid. Mom had been forced to go to extreme measures to get Claire's nose out of a book or head out of the clouds when it was homework time or dinner time or bath time. So it was only because of the screech of tires and a child's shrill scream that she was brought back to the present.

Was this the opportunity she'd been waiting for? The child screamed again. Then again, she hoped an innocent kid hadn't been hurt.

Forgetting her blistered feet, she dashed in the general direction of the sound and found a little girl standing in the middle of the street, crying her eyes out, with a car stopped mere inches from her. The little girl was trembling, obviously scared to death, and although there was a mob around her, apparently trying to comfort her, she wasn't consoled.

Her wet, drippy eyes focused on Claire and as Claire walked closer, the child ran toward her. *Bonnie! You little doll. You broke the rules again for me.* Claire knelt on the sidewalk, prepared to catch the scared little girl in her arms.

And then the child ran past her, calling, "Mommy! Mommy!"

"Oops." Now that was stupid. After glancing over her shoulder to make sure the kid had indeed found her mother, Claire stood up and continued down the street. What a silly thing to assume. Like that kid was going to come to her! A stranger! How dumb was that. Duh!

She chuckled at how stupid she must've looked and this time tried to concentrate on her surroundings instead of becoming lost in her thoughts. As she walked, she glanced in the windows of the shops she passed.

Sooner or later she was bound to run across someone who would need her help—if she wanted to wait an eternity. Obviously Bonnie wasn't going to drop a needy person in her lap. She was going to have to be a little more proactive.

She studied each person she passed, looking for her opportunity as she headed back toward the apartment. Finally, a promising subject came into view: a woman with one arm in a sling and the other full of baby boy. She was headed into a corner grocery store. Surely she'd need someone to help carry her parcels when she came out.

Feeling like a loitering criminal waiting for the right moment to pull off her heist, Claire paced back and forth in front of the store, waiting for the woman to emerge. It seemed like an eternity before she did, and when she stepped out onto the sidewalk, her plastic grocery bag hanging from her wrist, the baby in the same arm, Claire made a beeline for her. The minute the woman caught sight of her, however, she turned on her heel and headed back toward the store.

"Wait!" Claire said, not expecting the woman to actually listen.

The woman hesitated at the door, the handle gripped in her free hand, the one attached to her bum arm. She looked cautiously over her shoulder.

"I swear I'm not some creep out to steal your purse or baby or anything, despite my atrocious appearance."

The woman didn't move, nor did she give Claire any sort of encouragement to continue.

"I just wanted to help you out. I saw you go into the store—"

Without speaking a word, the woman threw open the door and plunged back inside the store.

Well, how was that for rude!

Claire followed her inside the store, saying to the woman's back, "I waited outside, figuring you'd have your hands full when you got out. And I was right."

"I'd like a half-pound of roast beef, please," the woman said to the clerk at the counter. She repositioned the baby, who seemed to be slowly sliding down toward her thigh.

"I'm not looking for money."

"Thank you," she said to the clerk as he handed her the wrapped meat. Her baby on her hip, her other arm in the sling, she awkwardly tried to shove the meat into her bag.

"I'd be happy to help you with that." Claire eyed the plastic bag's handle, which was starting to strain, thanks to the weight of whatever was inside.

"Darn it!" The wrapped meat slipped from the woman's fingers and landed with a dull thwack on the tile floor.

"Please, allow me. All I want to do is help you—" The bag's handle, stretched beyond its breaking point, snapped, and Claire lunged forward to catch the groceries before they hit the ground. The woman, no doubt thinking Claire was lunging at her, screamed, staggered backward, knocking her bum arm into a metal shelf full of canned vegetables, and fell to the ground. Her baby landed on her chest. Her hurt arm suddenly jutted straight down. It looked a little . . . wrong.

"Oh God!" Claire shouted. "What just happened?"

"My shoulder. It dislocated again when I tried to . . . oh!"

The baby started wailing. Claire started panicking. The

woman screamed again. A couple of shoppers gathered. General mayhem broke loose.

"Shoot! This is my fault." Claire kneeled next to the woman and set down her groceries. "I didn't mean to scare you. I shouldn't have moved so quickly but your bag was falling and I didn't want—"

The woman screamed again. The baby started wailing too.

"Should I call for help?" Claire asked, afraid to do anything.

"Someone, please call for help." The woman grimaced in pain. Her eyes were tightly clamped shut. "My baby. Please set him down on the floor next to me."

"Sure." Claire helped position the baby so it wouldn't fall or get hurt, then dashed through the store, asking everyone to call an ambulance. Gosh darn it, all she wanted to do was carry the woman's bag. Now she was the cause of a minor disaster! She returned to tell the woman the good news after she heard the store clerk say he'd called 911. "Help's on the way," she whispered.

"Ohhh . . . ouch, this hurts!"

Claire felt so hopeless watching the woman suffer. The baby was still crying. "Can I hold your baby for you? I promise I won't go anywhere."

"Ooh . . . ow!" she shrieked.

"I'll take that as a yes." Claire sat by the woman's side, cradling the blue-eyed baby in her arms until the ambulance arrived to take them both away.

Her eyes still shut, the woman gave Claire a slight smile between muscle spasms and said "Thank you." And then they were gone.

Now Claire was unsure. Had that counted as a kind deed, considering the woman's injury was partially—okay, mainly—her fault? She had helped her. She'd stood there for a long time and that baby had calmed, which let the woman suffer in peace. . . .

She stuffed her hand in the sweatshirt's front pocket and discovered a wad of paper. Curious, she drew it out. Money! Cold hard cash! Well, that answered her question. She could check off the good deed from her to-do list. It was done and now she had eight days and nights to do as she pleased.

Thank you, Bonnie!

It was past lunch time already and she was suffering from a serious case of missing Jake—his scent, his touch, his voice. If she didn't know better, she'd swear she was completely infatuated with the man already.

Fortunately, she knew she couldn't allow herself the luxury of even a mild case of infatuation. It would be senseless, foolish . . . plain stupid . . . to allow herself to develop any feelings for him beyond friendship and lust. Yeah, stupid.

She ran back to the apartment, anxious to see him.

As a man, Jake was accustomed to helping people with what resources he'd most often had at his disposal. Unfortunately, the one he used most—his large bank account—was not currently at his disposal, and he was left to find a more creative way to help someone. That made what should've been a simple task much more difficult.

Since he was not a small and unimposing guy—the nurses who worked for him used to tease him about scaring his pint-sized patients because he was so tall and dark—people tended to walk wide circles around him when they passed him on the street. He tried putting on a friendlier expression, an approach-me-I'm-a-good-guy smile, but it didn't help much.

As he made another circle around the block, he glanced down at his watch. Damn it! He'd told Claire he'd meet her back at the apartment over an hour ago. She had to think he'd skipped out on her. But never in a million years had he imagined he'd be walking in circles for over three hours trying to find anyone who would be willing to accept a small token of kindness from a stranger. The world had sure become a strange place, where even an offer to open a door was suspect.

An ambulance sped by and he watched for a moment, then turned right, heading north, vowing he'd stop in every open store he passed and look for someone who needed help. Anything—locked keys in the car, a hand with some groceries. Someone out there had to need his help!

He turned the corner and headed down a long city block lined on both sides with trendy clothing stores, delicatessens, and restaurants. If anywhere, this would probably be the best place to look. He walked into the first store, a shoe store, and glanced around for patrons. The store was empty so he tried the one next door, a deli.

There were a couple of ladies sitting at the counter, sipping coffee and chatting, probably on lunch break. One of them—a cute blonde—looked over her shoulder, gave him the eye, and then poked her friend's arm. The second woman, an equally attractive brunette, gave him a friendly come-on-over type of smile, and although he knew in his gut these two might be trouble, he walked toward them. He could handle them.

The blonde stood, then motioned him to take the bench to the left of the brunette. She sat on his other side so he was sandwiched between two temptresses. Years ago, he would've been in heaven sitting there with two very attractive, very willing women. But at the moment, there was only one woman he wanted, and she was probably back at the apartment, wondering where he'd run off to.

"Hi, ladies," he said casually.

"Hello there," Blondie said, not bothering to apologize for her wandering gaze as it took in every inch of his frame. He felt a little like a slab of prime beef in the butcher's window down the street. "I've been coming to this deli for almost ten years and I've never seen such a fine-looking man come in here. What's your name, sugar?"

"Jake. I'm just . . . er, passing through."

"How interesting," said the brunette, leaning a little closer.

"Where'd you come from?" asked Blondie, also shifting closer to him.

"Far away," he answered, feeling like he might have to peel these broads off his shoulders if they moved another inch. "I'm . . . uh . . . volunteering for a local charity and was wondering if either of you ladies could use a hand with anything? Carrying your"—he glanced down at the ground, hoping they'd have some shopping bags sitting at their feet, which they didn't— "bags? Jump starting your car?"

"You've already jump started my engine," said the brunette in a purr. She dropped a hand in his lap and he felt his eyes bugging from his head.

Damn, these girls meant business!

But he was not interested. No way. He grabbed her hand, gently removed it from his groin, and stood. "Okay. Well, guess I'd better go find someone else who could use a little bit of charity—"

"Wait," Blondie said before he'd gotten any farther than a step. "I apologize for my friend's obnoxious behavior. Neither one of us normally acts this way. We had a little bet going and unfortunately for you, you were the first decent, friendly-looking guy to walk in here. Anyway, I could use some help with some firewood, if you're still offering. I live just around the block."

"Really?" he asked, hoping this wasn't some kind of a trick.

"Honest. Cross my heart and hope to die." She crossed her chest with a bright red-nailed fingertip.

"Don't say that," he said.

That comment earned him some puzzled expressions from both women, which he didn't mind. For one, it beat the I'm-going-to-eat-you-alive stares they'd first given him.

"Anyway," Blondie said, "You can follow us. We walked but if you're driving—"

"I walked too. Staying with a friend not too far from here."

"Good. Then you can walk us home. You aren't some crazy rapist, are you?"

"No. But having me walk you home after just meeting me probably isn't a smart move."

"Tell me about it. But for some reason, I trust you. Call me crazy." She opened her purse, plopped a few bills on the counter—no doubt to pay her tab—then stood. He hustled to the door to let them out but as he pushed it open for them and followed them out, he ran smack dab into Claire, who looked shocked to find him there.

Speechless—because he could just imagine how it looked, him standing sandwiched between a couple of babes—he pointed down the street. "I . . . uh. My errand took a little longer than expected but I'll be back at the apartment in a few."

"I see," Claire said flatly. Then her expression changed. She smiled. It wasn't a stunner of a grin, more the kind of smile one gives when they're posing for the fiftieth photograph at a wedding. "I just came up here to get a cola." Her gaze hopped back and forth between him and the girls.

He felt like a jerk but there was no use trying to explain now. He hoped she'd give him a chance later. "I just need to lug some firewood in for this woman and I'll be home. Okay?"

The two girls huddled closer, whispering to each other as they eyeballed Claire, which only made him feel worse for her.

"Okay." She brushed by him and went inside. Silently rehearsing his explanation, he followed the girls down the street.

Chapter 9

"I know how it looked—"

Almost a full hour after she'd bumped into Jake at the deli, an hour of quiet self-chastisement and a few tears, Claire smiled reassuringly at him. "You don't owe me an explanation." Wow. If she didn't know better, she'd actually believe she meant that.

"But I want to—"

"I found a video store down the street and rented *Braveheart*. Want to watch it with me?" She carried a plate heaped with extra-crispy fried chicken, tossed salad, and greasy, naughty, totally delicious roasted potatoes to the coffee table, then sat down on the couch. Not staying alive for more than nine days every ten years had one benefit: at least she could eat anything she liked without having to worry about gaining weight. She couldn't remember the last time she'd been free to eat anything she liked. Probably not since she'd graduated from kindergarten. "There's more chicken if you want some. Are you hungry?"

"Yeah . . ." He looked at her for a moment, then went to the kitchen and fixed his plate. Moments later, still looking as perplexed as he did when he left, he sat beside her.

She hit the remote button, starting the video. "I've been waiting forever for this movie to come out."

"It was released almost ten years ago. I saw it at the movie theater." He gave her an odd look, then shoveled a forkful of salad into his mouth.

"Yeah. I . . . er, just never got around to renting it. And I hate movie theaters. Sitting in dark, crowded rooms with a bunch of strangers. And gum glued to the chairs. Yuck!"

"I hear you," he said around a mouthful. "It's a damn good movie. Sad. I hated it when the English guys killed the man's wife—"

She swatted him on the arm before he had a chance to spill any more of the plot. "Shut up! So, you're one of those people who have to tell the whole story and ruin it for the poor schmucks who are watching it with you. Don't tell me . . . you also memorize the dialogue."

"Only from movies I've seen more than once or twice. I watched this one only once, so you're safe . . . at least from me boring you with recitations of *Braveheart* dialogue. I can't say the same about *Star Wars*. I watched that one a lot." He grinned and she couldn't help laughing. He was really such a goof.

"But seriously—this is a very depressing movie. So if you have need of a shoulder to cry on, I have one handy right here." He patted the shoulder closest to her.

"Thanks. I'll remember that."

And she did, over and over. In the beginning, when Mel's blue-eyed character was a kid at his father's funeral. And again, when his wife and he sneaked into the woods to get married. And again, when his wife was killed. And again, when he was tortured. . . .

By the end, her stomach was full, her eyes burning, her heart heavy, and her mood glum, yet she felt warm and close and cozy and cared for. As the credits played, she looked at Jake and sighed. "You weren't kidding. That was easily the most depressing movie I've ever seen. Thanks for helping me through it."

"My pleasure. How about we go for a walk?" he suggested with smiling eyes that spoke volumes and made her want to stay curled up against him for the next ten years.

"Sure. But I want to change first. I bought some clothes while I was out." It took great effort to remove herself from that spot on the couch, but she managed. She put her plate in the dishwasher and the rest of the leftover food in the fridge, then went into the torture chamber, which was looking less scary each visit she paid to it, and changed into a pair of clean undies and bra. A pair of well-fitting jeans, a T-shirt, and some comfortable shoes and she was all set. Much better! After putting on some makeup and fixing her hair, she trotted out to the living room, feeling like a million bucks. Funny what some decent-fitting clothes and Maybelline could do for a girl.

He clearly appreciated her efforts to make herself more presentable. With a grin the size of Texas, he said, "On second thought, maybe we should stay in." He crossed the room in two long strides and wrapped his arms around her in a warm bear hug.

Very glad she'd been able to talk herself out of being upset about those women earlier, she smiled and sank into his embrace. To shake her earlier funk, she'd had to repeat, "He's not mine. I have no right. He's not mine. I have no right." It must've taken at least a thousand times before she felt a little bit better.

Now, after having his arms around her and his gravelly voice whispering comforting words in her ear, she felt like the only woman on earth. Even so, jumping back in the sack didn't hit her the right way. Not yet. She wanted more talk time before getting to the bump and grind.

She wriggled free, knowing if she didn't get a little distance between them soon, she'd be saying "to heck with the walk" and leaping back into bed. "As tempting as your proposition is, I'd rather go for a walk first. After eating all that chicken, I feel like a bloated whale. Besides, you've got me all geared up for a walk," she said, trying to sound upbeat, knowing some men didn't take rejection well, not that she was totally rejecting him.

"And seeing you like this has got me all geared up for something else." He winked. Before she could do a thing, he caught her upper arms in his fists and lowered his head for a kiss.

"Wait." She pressed two flat palms against a chest that felt like concrete—very attractive concrete under white cotton with just a sprinkling of hair . . ."Oh . . ." she murmured as her mouth joined his. His tongue, teeth, and lips made her forget whatever she was about to say. Her insides simmered. Her legs grew wobbly and weak, like when she'd first reanimated, which provided the perfect excuse for her to wrap her arms around his neck and press closer to him.

She'd fall down otherwise.

She felt a telltale lump against her belly and knew where they were headed. That realization only spiked her temperature higher until eventually she was swimmy-headed, breathless, and dizzy.

He broke the kiss and muttered, "You really are something, Claire. I'm so glad you didn't jump to any conclusions about those women."

Did he have to mention that now? Pretending not to mind the fact that they were groin-to-groin but discussing two gorgeous women with perfect hair and perfect faces and, from the looks of things, perfect boobs.

"I mean, most women would've been pissed off and thrown footwear at me, or something equally pain-inducing, and then stormed off."

"The only footwear I had at the moment was secured to my feet," she said dryly.

"Then you were mad?"

"No." She took a giant step backward, then motioned toward the door. "How about that walk now? I . . . uh . . . wanted to buy . . ." She glanced at the calendar hanging on the wall. It was Halloween night! There'd be trick-or-treaters knocking on the door within the hour. "Candy! For the kids."

"Good idea." He pulled open the door and looked down at her as she squeezed by him. "So, you're not mad. Right? I just want to make sure, since we don't have a whole lot of time together."

"Right. Because we don't have a whole lot of time together," she said, not waiting for him to close the door before skipping down the stairs and heading out onto the sidewalk below. It was a whole lot easier descending that steep staircase in tennis shoes that fit properly.

"Wow. Can I say that?" he asked as he fell into step beside her. They headed up the block, toward a store she'd seen earlier on the corner.

"Sure."

"Wow," he repeated. "I mean . . . wow. You're so understanding."

"You already said that."

"I know. But wow. You're really something special. I only wish I hadn't waited until now . . ."

"Yeah. Me too," she confessed.

"You were engaged." He sounded surprised.

As she glanced at him, she saw he looked surprised too. Why would that surprise him? Didn't he know how adorable he was? How sexy and sweet he was? What an amazing find he was? "Are you kidding me?" she asked. "I would've broken up with Matt in a minute if I'd known—" she forced herself not to finish that sentence. It wasn't fair to Jake. It wasn't fair to her. I wasn't fair to anyone to continue down that road. There was no time for regrets and should-haves.

They went into the store and bought a bag of every kind of candy they could find. Ever the gentleman, Jake insisted on carrying the bag. They held hands, and Claire knew as they walked she had the goofiest grin on her face but she couldn't help it.

Extremely happy, Claire tried to stow away every moment in her memory, every sensation. The air smelled crisp, of fall and leaves and grass. It was cool but not cold, just the perfect temperature, and the sky was clear. To the west, the sun had just dropped behind the buildings.

His hand was warm in hers. Warm and big and comforting and she didn't ever want to let it go.

They returned to the apartment and Claire filled a bowl with candy. She stationed herself at the foot of the front stairs, right next to the sidewalk. Jake sat at her side, his wide frame practically filling the entire front stoop, and chatted with her between kids. They both oohed and aahed over the clever costumes and chuckled when a little child toddled up, barely able to walk, let alone say, "trick or treat."

When it seemed like the last stragglers had been served, they carried the remaining candy upstairs, shut the door, and looked at each other.

"They were cute, weren't they?" she asked, feeling her face flush. She carried the bowl into the kitchen and set it on the table.

"Adorable."

"I wonder sometimes what my kids might've looked like." She unwrapped a bite-sized candy bar and popped it into her mouth. Chocolatey goodness! Yummy!

"Might've? You don't want to have kids?" He reached around her and scooped a fistful of candy, then took her hand in his and led her to the living room.

"I . . . can't have kids," she admitted with genuine regret.

"Sorry." He hesitated before adding, "I can't either."

He stepped closer, so close she could smell his leather jacket. So close, she could see the tiny lines fanning from his blue, blue eyes and the tiny flecks of gold in their sky-hued depth.

"We have a lot in common," she whispered, her breath catching in her throat.

"Yeah." He set the candy on the coffee table, then drew her into his arms.

This time she didn't resist in the least. Nor did she try to stop him when he kissed her. The whole day—at least after the twin-babe incident—had been so romantic. It'd been the best day she'd had in a long, long time.

She'd had chocolate. She'd had a great movie and deep-fried food. The only thing left to top off her day was some more sex. Sex with a gorgeous, kind, gentle man who seemed to know what to say and do to make her feel special—well, at least most of the time.

And this kiss, this mind-melting, toe-curling kiss was a good start to a wonderful evening. His hands started at her neck but before long wandered to her breasts, her stomach, her butt.

All too soon, he pulled away and looked at her through heavy-lidded eyes burning with hunger. "How about going into the bedroom?"

"Sure. Okay."

He took her hand and led her into the bedroom. This time, he took his time undressing her. He kissed and nipped every inch of skin he uncovered as he removed her shirt and pants. He unclasped her bra, then gave her breasts more attention than they'd had in her entire life. He sucked and nibbled, kneaded and stroked each one until her back was arched and her chest was pushed up high in the air. Her breathing rasped inside her head and she blindly reached out to grasp any part of him she could touch. Her fingers tangled in silky curls on the top of his head.

Just when she thought she couldn't take another moment of the sweet torture he was so generously lavishing over her breasts, he stopped and inched slowly south, trailing soft butterfly kisses down her stomach. When he reached her groin, he shifted his weight, freeing her legs, then gently pushed them apart.

Oh! He was going to . . . ohhhh . . . She dropped her head back and closed her eyes.

When he parted her folds with his fingers, then ran his hot tongue down her slit, she nearly melted. Then that amazingly agile tongue found her sensitive nub and danced lightly over it until her heartbeat pounded in her ears and every muscle in her body was tense. She felt the heat from her cheeks sliding like silk down her body. She gasped.

"Are you going to?" he asked, sounding as breathless as she was.

"Yes."

"Don't."

"Why not?"

"Because."

Oh! She was there, teetering on the cusp of orgasm. "Then you better stop doing what you're doing, buddy," she said, not really paying any attention to what she was saying.

"Okay." He stopped.

"Don't stop!" She lifted her swimmy head and opened her eyes. What a sight, his face between her parted legs. It was almost enough to finish the job. Not quite, though.

"I have a surprise for you," he said with a rough, gravelly, having-sex kind of voice.

"Oh?"

"Wait here." He got up and ran to the closet holding all the scary whips and stuff. After rummaging around for a few minutes, he returned with something small and pink. He held it up for her to see. "What do you think of these?"

"Think of them? What are they?" Were those . . . pink fur handcuffs? How cute! "Oh . . ."

"Look, they come with a friend." He held up a second pair. "And wouldn't you know it, there are loops up here on the headboard for them to lock onto."

"Imagine that," she joked.

"Wanna give them a test run?"

You don't have to ask me twice. "Uh . . . sure. But first, tell me you have the key, right? Because you always see on sitcoms how someone gets locked up with handcuffs and they can't find the key."

"You don't need one for these." He held the silver and pink gadget up to her face and pointed at a little clippy-looking lever thing next to the lock slit. "See this? It unlocks them without the keys."

"Okay."

"Excellent!" Before he'd finished the word, he had her left arm secured in the first handcuff. He latched it to the headboard, then worked on the other wrist. She wriggled her arms a little, testing the cuffs. The pink fur tickled her wrists and she giggled.

"Be right back." He dashed back to the little closet of horrors and returned a moment later with a metal bar and the stick with tickly fringe she'd admired yesterday. "Are you willing to try a couple other things?"

"They won't hurt me, right? Because I can tell you with some certainty that I'm not into pain." She was oh-so-aware of the fact that her arms were spread out and up. It completely turned her on. Her stomach muscles were rhythmically contracting, lifting her pelvis up then lowering it, up then lowering it, like they did when he was kissing her out of her mind.

He licked his lips and explained, holding up the metal bar. "This is a spreader."

"A spreader," she repeated a little louder than she'd intended.

"Yes. It holds your legs apart. These straps go around

your thighs. They're soft so there's no pain involved. Just a sense of loss of control."

"Loss of control . . ."

"Would you like to try it?"

She shook her head. "I don't think so. Not yet."

"That's okay." He set the spreader on the floor and parted her legs with his hands. Wow, what a feeling! Her arms spread wide, her legs held apart. Her sex was throbbing, dripping, clenching. Her breathing was ragged and loud. Her entire body was all tingley and jittery.

"Mmmm," he said, admiring her. His gaze caressed her body, making her even hotter. After having come so close to an orgasm and now with the handcuffs making her even hornier, her body was screaming for completion. "You look delicious. I could sit here and stare at you all day."

"All day? Oh, please don't do that."

"What's wrong, love?"

"Oh . . . nothing. I'm just tied to this bed . . . and I might need to . . . well, take care of some personal issues sometime down the road."

He chuckled. The deep, rumbly sound did even more damage to her fraying nerves. He leaned forward, way, way low, until his breath warmed her neck. "Okay. I'll set a time limit."

"Okay," she half-spoke, half-gasped.

"One last thing," he whispered in her ear. "This is a tickler." He held up the last piece he'd extracted from the torture closet and combed his fingers through the fringe. "This part tickles. Would you like to try it?"

"Okay," she said on a huff.

"You're being such a good girl, you deserve a reward. Look at you . . ."

"Yeah . . ."

". . . so open and willing and eager to please me."

"Yeah."

He ran the tickler down the cleft between her breasts,

then circled one nipple. Instinctively, she arched her back to try to thrust her breast higher, but with her arms held up and out as they were, that wasn't easy.

She really had no control. None. He had complete control over her. Oh, this was strange. No, wonderful!

No, strangely wonderful.

"What are you thinking?" He ran the tickler down her stomach and between her legs, which made her gasp so sharply her head swam.

"I'm thinking . . ." That naughty little tickler traveled lower, teasing her bottom, and her eyes closed, her breath caught in her throat, and she wasn't able to finish her sentence.

"Yes?"

"I'm not thinking."

"That's good." The tickler disappeared, replaced by lips and tongue. He pushed two fingers inside her, bending them just so, creating the most incredible friction. With two inward thrusts and a few flickers of that tongue, she was once again in the throes of ecstasy.

She tried to writhe but couldn't. So instead she just said, "Oh my God, oh my God, ohmygod!"

It was close, right there . . . yes, oh yes!

He stopped again, dragging his fingers out of her just before her passage spasmed around them. "Not, yet love."

"Grrr!" She blinked open her eyes.

He didn't smile and he didn't look particularly comfortable either. Good! For all this torture he deserved a little discomfort too. "I want to feel your climax as your sweet folds milk me."

"Please . . ." She dropped her head back and closed her eyes again, waiting impatiently for him to decide when he'd let her have her well-deserved release. This loss-of-control thing had its drawbacks!

She heard the soft rustle of cotton over rock-hard man as he removed his pants, shirt, and boxers, and in a heartbeat, she felt his weight pressing on the mattress directly in front of her dripping-wet sex.

"I wish this could last forever," he murmured.

"I don't. I'm dying here."

"Patience, sweet. You'll get what you've been waiting for."

She tensed slightly when she felt his first touch to her privates. His rod begged entrance into her tight slit as his fingers ran up and down, up and down. And when it plunged home in one stroke, his fingers danced over her nub.

She moaned some incomprehensible gibberish that sounded like "mfrgh . . . oh . . . glifflegag . . ."—she had no idea what she'd wanted so say—then yanked at the handcuffs holding her wrists up over her head.

"That's it, baby. Oh, yes. You're so hot." He continued to thrust, in and out, in and out, while his fingers did things magical and wonderful to her whole body. And then she felt another finger pressing at her back entry.

"Oh no!" She tensed.

"It's okay. You're so wet and ready." His voice sounded strained, like an anaconda was wrapped around his chest, squeezing. "I'm just going to touch," he said, his big, rigid, wonderful thick hardness still thrusting in and out of her. To illustrate, he pressed that finger just slightly, only a fraction of an inch. Her thigh muscles trembled in response and she felt herself once again soaring toward a powerful orgasm.

She sucked in a breath and held it.

"Oh, yeah. Oh, yeah. So sweet and hot," he murmured, hammering in and out now, his finger sliding up and down along her crack. "Oh, baby. I'm going to come."

Those words sent her over the edge. She was swept up in an orgasm so powerful she'd swear her teeth were spasming. And she felt her pulsing sex milking his thick member as he growled a low groan and slowed his thrusting.

Her orgasm went on and on, pulse after pulse, spasm after spasm, draining every cell in her body of tension until she was a limp mass of goo.

Then she sighed.

He pulled out and dropped to rest beside her. He threw an arm over her chest, his arm hair tickling her nipples and making them hard. "Sweet Jesus," he repeated in her ear. "Dear, sweet Jesus."

"Praying? Now?"

"Hell yes! I swear I just saw heaven."

Chapter 10

Claire woke up with a start and looked at the clock. She had a half hour—thirty short minutes—to get dressed and walk clear across town. Shoot! And she had no wheels. Did the busses run at close to midnight? She couldn't afford to be late. The need to find answers to the questions that had been haunting her for nine years wouldn't allow it.

Trying hard not to wake Jake as she moved—not easy considering half his body was draped over hers—she wiggled and squirmed out from under his bulk and rolled to the edge of the bed.

"Where are you going?" he asked her back.

Darn it! How would she explain a midnight run like freaking Cinderella's? "I um . . . had a craving?" *And my chariot's going to turn into a pumpkin.*

"Now?"

"Yep. It's a female thing. You know. PMS cravings. They're a killer, especially in the middle of the night. You're so lucky you're a man."

"Oka-a-ay," he said doubtfully. "Do you want me to go out and get you something? Some chocolate maybe? Or ice cream?"

"No. I wouldn't want to make you go to all that trouble. I'll get it myself. Besides, a craving is a subjective thing. I need to pick out what I want. If you got the wrong thing, it could spell disaster."

"No, really," he insisted. "Let me. Please. I need to . . . um, pick something up from the store myself."

"No," she said, fumbling in the dark for the light. She banged herself on one of the torture devices and let out a surprised yelp.

"Yes," he insisted. "I'll go." A light switched on, illuminating Jake's whisker-coated face. Wow. They made him look dangerous and masculine and oh so yummy! "Why are you arguing with me?"

"Because . . . I have to go out and get something else too." she reasoned, knowing what his next question would be.

"What?"

"Something personal and that's all I'm going to say." At last locating her clothes, she dressed, then made a beeline for the door. "Don't wait up for me. I'll be gone a while—I think. And don't worry. I'll be fine."

"Why the mystery?" Still rumpled and smelling of sex, he caught her by the elbow just before she walked out.

"Because there are some things that are hard to explain and this is one of them. We women are a mystery. What can I say? Um. Sorry for waking you up, though." She glanced over his shoulder at the clock on the wall. She'd just wasted almost ten minutes! If she was going to stand any chance of getting to her destination on time, she had to leave. Pronto! "Gotta go. Now. Be back soon." Knowing she owed him more but afraid to take more time to explain now, she kissed him quickly and dashed out of the apartment.

Even though she felt weak and trembly and tired, she didn't stop running for quite a while. She ran toward the main drag through town, Center Street, then turned right. Her former fiancé's place was about two miles away. Two miles in twenty minutes. Okay, that wasn't impossible, if you were a freakin' marathon runner! Practically doubled over from stomach cramps, she slowed to a fast walk.

She noticed as she shuffled down the street—which even at this hour had a fair amount of traffic, including an occasional pedestrian—that no one was looking at her. She attributed the heavier-than-normal traffic to it being Halloween night. But why people seemed to be staring clear through her, she had no notion—that was, until she got to Matt's house.

The first thing she did was check the name on the mailbox. He still lived there. Why did that not surprise her? The man had always been steady, resistant to change, even difficult to talk into a new haircut. Of course he hadn't moved.

Although she knew that even if he was home he wouldn't likely answer the door, she knocked anyway and waited.

Nothing.

His lack of response left her with few options, breaking in being one of them. Since she didn't favor spending the rest of her eight days in jail, she tried knocking again, this time harder. And called out, "Hey, Matt! I know you're in there. Open up. Ple-e-e-ease."

Like he was going to respond to that. Not.

She reached out for the doorknob, figuring before she did anything rash she'd check and see if he was still in the habit of leaving the front door unlocked. For a guy who craved security he was mighty lax with the front door and unfortunately it had led to tragedy. Had he learned a lesson?

Before she twisted it, she heard someone on the other side fumbling with the lock. Evidently, he did lock it now. Well, good for him! At least her demise hadn't been in vain.

He pulled open the door and she couldn't help noticing he'd aged considerably since she'd last seen him. His head was as shiny and bald as an egg-hued bowling ball. Wow. And quite a few lines etched his face. "Hello?" he said.

Spent a lot of time in the sun the past few years, have ya? She cleared her throat. "Hi! I . . . was in the neighborhood—"

"Hello?" He poked his hairless head out farther and looked to the right, then the left, shrugged his shoulders and slammed the door. In her face!

"Wha—? Jerk! Act like you can't see me." Not fond of being treated like she was invisible, even if she was the man's ex-fiancé and probably the last person on earth he wanted to see at close to midnight, she knocked again, harder.

Obviously, he was waiting on the other side of the door, because it flew open mid-knock. He stared straight at her again. "Who's doing that?" he asked, sounding exasperated and angry.

"Me!" She waved her arms in front of his nose. "Right here. Whoo-hoo!"

"Darn it, whoever's doing that, I'm going to call the cops if it happens again. Darn kids," he grumbled. ". . . hate freaking Halloween." He reached for the door with one gangly arm and was clearly intending to shut it again, in her face, but this time she inched by his newly acquired potbelly into the house.

He slammed the door and turned around.

"So, you aren't going to say a word? Not a 'Hey, how's it going?' or 'What the hell are you doing here? You're dead!' or 'Wow, you look terrific'?" she asked, blocking him from heading down the hallway.

He didn't stop. Instead, he walked right by her, all tired and grumbling, like there wasn't a dead woman standing in the center of his foyer.

What was his problem? Did he think if he ignored her she'd go away?

She followed him down the hall to the bedroom, figuring she had to go there anyway. Yes, it was weird seeing him after all this time. He had aged a lot in nine years; didn't look much like the man she'd been engaged to. And his feeble attempt at pretending she wasn't there wasn't making this any less awkward, but it was, unfortunately, necessary if she was going to be around for the next few days, not to mention if she was going to find out exactly what happened nine years ago.

"So, since you're not going to ask me—which, by the way I don't get—how are things hanging with you?" She took in his ratty pajamas, shrunken appendages, swollen belly, hair-free head, and deeply lined face and said flatly, "You look . . . go-o-o-o-od . . ."

Instead of responding to her kind compliment, he silently shuffled back into the bedroom, sat on the edge of the bed, and grunted as he slid off his hole-pocked slippers.

She sat next to him, not sure if she had to actually—ack!—lay down where she'd died. Out of nerves, or annoyance, she couldn't be sure which, she chattered, "You know, you're missing a great opportunity here. If I saw a dead person—especially someone who died in bed with me!—I'd be keeping them busy answering questions, like, 'What's it like to die?' or 'Is heaven really as great as they say?' or 'Can you watch what everyone's doing on earth when you're up there?' or 'Did you happen to meet Elvis?' "

He lay down, rolled away from her, punched the pillow, then settled his head on it.

"So that's how you're going to be? Just pretend the dead girl isn't there and she'll go back to hell or wherever she came from." She tapped his shoulder and he shrugged away from her touch. "Like it or not, I'm not leaving. At least not yet. So talk to me!"

No response.

"Okay. You're asking for it, buddy. Darn it, you were never this stubborn or childish . . ."—*Or so poorly groomed!*—". . . before. But I still miss you, you goof." She briefly considered her options, then belted out, "Memories! Like the corners of my mind . . ."

No response.

"Misty water-colored memmmmories . . . of the way we were."

No response.

"Okay. You wanna be that way, we don't have to talk right now. I can wait a few minutes. I'm feeling kind of crappy now anyway. Sorry to see you're still sleeping alone. Hope that's not because of me, though you don't seem to be exactly thrilled to see me." Nauseated and frustrated, she lay down next to him, smack-dab on the spot she'd died.

Wow, did it feel creepy being there, with his soft snores buzzing like a fly in her ear, almost like nine years hadn't passed and time had stood still—except for, of course, the way he looked.

Not sure what to expect, she stared at the dark ceiling overhead and waited for something to happen. Would some bolt shoot from the sky and go into her body? Would she levitate? Or maybe just tingle all over?

When nothing happened, she sat up. The bedsprings squeaked.

The sound evidently made Matt startle. He sat up, blinking in the dark, and swiveled his head back and forth. "Who's there?"

"Now you're just plain being mean. Would you quit pretending I'm not sitting right here—" She patted the mattress and the springs squeaked again.

He jerked like someone had just lit a match under his butt. "Who's doing that?"

"What? This?" She hit the mattress a couple more times and he sailed from the bed.

"Holy shit!" he screeched, stumbling backward.

Even in the dark, Claire could see his chest heaving and

his pupils dilating in terror. Either he had become an Oscar-caliber actor in the past nine years, or he was seriously scared.

"Whoo-hoo! It's okay. I'm not going to do anything too scary, like mess with your monthly budget . . . again." She stood and walked to the light and flipped it on. "Here, maybe in the light you'll see it's me. This time."

"Holy shit!" he yelled again, backing into the corner like a scared ninny in a bad hacker film. "Who the hell is doing that?"

She almost found him laughable, standing in the corner, trembling like a blade of grass in a hurricane, the front of his drawstring pajama pants stained dark—ew! "Jesus. You wet yourself? Been having some prostate problems lately too?"

He kept looking around the room, like he couldn't see her, even with the blazing light of nearly a dozen halogen ceiling pot lights at full illumination.

He couldn't see her? Why the heck not? Everyone else had been able to. And she could still do stuff, like flip on lights and make mattresses bounce? Huh. Testing her abilities, she flipped the light on and off a few times, which only made Matt more freaked out.

She had to admit, it was making her a little freaked out too.

When had she become invisible? She ran across the room to the mirror to see if she'd see her reflection. In the process, she kicked the bench at the foot of the bed, stubbing her big toe, even through her shoe. She yelped in pain and hopped up and down as the magazines stacked on the bench fell to the floor.

"Holy shit!" Matt said again.

He was saying that a lot at the moment. Before tonight she'd never heard him say anything more colorful than "shoot" or maybe an occasional "poop."

Okay. Now what? She was in a room with a man

who'd just wet himself. And she had to be there, couldn't leave. And she had to do something—whatever that might be—so she could enjoy another week with Jake. And she was dying to ask Matt a bunch of questions but it seemed he couldn't hear her either. And . . . and . . . wow, this was weird.

Matt was now inching his way toward the phone, no doubt ready to call the police. But what would he say to them? There was an invisible person shaking his bed?

She chuckled. "It sucks being you." Then, "Sorry. That was mean."

He picked up the phone and put it to his ear but he didn't dial. Then he slammed it back down. "Damn it, if I call the police they're bound to just call the guys in the white coats."

"You got that right."

"I have to be just imagining things. Or it's a short in the wires. Yeah. Kids were playing pranks at the front door. And a short in the wires is making the lights flicker. And the magazines were sitting on the edge of the bench . . . and the mattress . . . uh, the mattress . . . and that smell in the bed." He made a funny face, wrinkled his nose. "That god-awful stench."

"Hey, now you're getting personal."

"Maybe a mouse died under the bed." He walked to the bed and stooped over to take a peek underneath it.

"I showered this morning! I don't smell like dead rodents." She checked her armpits, then her breath. Neither stank to her. They didn't exactly smell like roses but they didn't reek like decaying animal flesh either. "Okay. So maybe I could use a Tic Tac, but your morning breath is far worse."

"Nothing under there. Maybe in the bed." He pulled the sheets back and screamed like a girl. Not just "Eek!" but "Eeeeeeek!" and jumped back from the bed.

Sounds like he found the source of the smell. And it

wasn't me, thank you very much. Curious, she stepped closer.

On the sheets was a huge red stain. Looked like blood. And ho boy was the stench awful.

Wonder why I didn't smell it earlier. I was lying right there.

The weird thing, she noticed as she stared at it a little longer, was the shape. The stain was shaped like a person—a small one at that. Not exactly kid sized, but the height of a small adult. Head on the pillowcase, then shoulders, two arms, torso, legs. Creepy!

Had someone else died in that bed recently? If so, where was the body? Or the ghost?

"Oh my God! Claire?" Matt said into the air, spinning round and round like a top about to teeter over.

"Yes. It's me! Can you see me? Finally!" She waved her arms around like a big lame bird trying to take flight.

"Are you here? If you are, I swear I didn't know they'd do this to you. I swear. Please! Please don't hurt me. I mean I was a shit and I deserve it. But I'm very, very sorry."

She stopped flapping. "You're sorry? What?" she asked aloud. "What the heck are you talking about?" His confession was strange. Scary, actually. Had she misunderstood or had he just admitted he'd known the men who'd killed her?

How was that possible? She thought those men had been burglars.

Burglars who'd walked in the freaking unlocked front door—how many times had she told him that was dangerous—and demanded he hand over the chunk of change he kept in his top dresser drawer. Of all the stupid things to do! Keeping, like, freaking thousands of dollars in cash in your house. Duh!

Who ever heard of not trusting a bank? At least since the Great Depression. Hello! That's what the Federal Reserve was for . . . or was it the FDIC?

"Oh, God, oh God! What have I done?" he sniveled, dropping on his knees on the floor and running his hands over the stained sheet. Blood seemed to be oozing from it, coating his hands, arms, chest, face.

It was gross. It was scary. It was damn confusing and it was the last thing she'd expected to happen.

These weren't the answers she'd been waiting to hear!

What was going on?

Chapter 11

Jake stood at the gaping front door, watching Claire run like a scared rabbit down the street. Had she found out the truth? That she was sleeping with a corpse? Darn it! He knew he should've told her sooner.

Grumbling to himself, he closed the door, found some clothes, and got dressed. The timing of her hasty departure was convenient anyway, since he had to get down to the railroad crossing in the next twenty minutes or so. Luckily it wasn't far, about a mile away.

Dressed, and already missing Claire's smile—he wondered if he would see it again—he walked toward the intersection where he'd had his accident. There was a lot more traffic out than usual, and that was saying something since it was Friday night. It was warm for late fall, so there were groups of teens roaming the streets, dressed in their ghoulish costumes, passing burning cigarettes back and forth and looking for trouble. None of them gave him a second glance.

Turning, he headed down the familiar stretch of road he'd traveled every morning on his way to the office. When he approached the spot, which of course showed no signs of the tragedy that had happened just over nine years ago, he stopped and looked around. What the hell was he supposed to do now? It wasn't like they'd given him an instruction pamphlet on how to do this. Damn spiritual bureaucrats. Created a shitload of paperwork, then just tossed a spirit out there in the world to figure out what the heck he was supposed to do on his own.

Guess I wait.

He stepped into the exact spot where he'd been parked when the train had derailed, stood in the middle of the stinking road like a possum waiting to become road kill, and watched for signs from above.

A white glob of poop landed on his shoulder. Darned pigeons! He looked up. "That wasn't exactly the sign I was expecting. Want to give me a clue what to do here before I'm killed again?"

A light flashed in the corner of his eye and with dread he spun around, just in time to see the blazing headlights of a car headed straight at him.

"Shit!" he shouted when he realized the driver was not going to stop. He leapt out of the way mere seconds before joining the flattened raccoon in the left lane. "What the hell's wrong with you, asshole?" he shouted after the car. It hadn't slowed a bit. Homicidal jerk!

Then he recognized he'd been at fault too. Standing in the middle of the road—where cars and trucks could legally travel—in the pitch black was about the dumbest thing a guy could do, at least if he didn't want to be flattened under a Suburban.

But what the hell? The rules were the rules and his caseworker had told him he had to return to the exact place where he'd expired.

Getting impatient real fast, he stepped back into position, making sure to keep an eye on traffic. Still, nothing happened. No energy beams or sparks or even little static zaps. And then he thought about it for a moment.

His memory of that day was sketchy at best but he recalled waking up disoriented and lightheaded in his truck.

He remembered the screech of pulled metal and the voices of firefighters as they worked to get him out of his flattened truck.

Maybe he hadn't perished in his truck, but somewhere else. He walked back, in the opposite direction, away from the tracks, and noticed a dark spot on the side of the road. It was large, at least six feet long. He hadn't noticed it when he'd walked past this spot earlier.

Figuring he had nothing to lose, he stepped closer. It was dark, hard to make out the details, but as he stared at it, he could tell it was changing somehow. While at first it had looked flattened, like an oil stain on the gravel shoulder, now it looked three dimensional, like a . . . person?

It sat up and Jake leapt back, shouting, "What the hell?" Then, in the blink of an eye, it shot through the air and landed on him and his whole body was ablaze in sensual, intoxicating heat.

Claire's head was seriously spinning and she had no idea if it was because she needed to recharge or because of the unbelievable crap coming out of her ex-fiancé's mouth. Probably a little of both.

". . . I swear I wouldn't have done this if I'd known how it would've turned out . . . I loved you . . . I never wanted you to get hurt," he said through sobs and sniffles.

"I feel sick." Unable to stand anymore, she sat next to him on the bed, rested her elbows on her knees, and dropped her chin in her hands. "If those weren't your average run-of-the-mill-burglars who the heck were they?"

"I'm so-o-o-o sorry. I swear. I deserve to go to hell for this . . . oh . . ."

"You're not going to answer me, are you?"

"Oh, Jesus, what have I done? How can I make this better? What can I do?"

"You could start by telling me what the heck happened, dumb jerk!" she said, unable to hold her anger in check anymore. "Would you quit babbling and tell me what happened? Why the hell did I get murdered!" So angry she did the one thing that really pissed her off—crying—she dropped back on the bed and let the tears fly. The bed springs shrieked as she dropped onto the mattress and Matt screamed again, then wailed louder, like a little future-wife-murdering coward.

Damn it, she hated to cry! Damn it, she hated the sound of his blabbering. Damn it, she'd thought tonight would be awkward but . . . but not like this! Not shocking and scary and awful! Her future husband had been the cause of her death. Somehow. The man she had thought she'd known but obviously didn't. But she couldn't get the pant-peeing bastard to tell her how he was responsible.

Well, shoot! Now she had to know the truth but how would she find out? She wasn't a Charlie's freaking Angel or Mrs. stinking King or Agatha goddamn Christie. She needed help . . . from someone. Someone she could trust.

Okay, after learning she hadn't known her fiancé after dating him for five years, there weren't too many people she trusted at the moment. *Better start a little lower on the scale.* She needed someone who would believe her. And when said someone found out the truth, he would break it to her gently. She couldn't handle any more shockers like this one.

There was only one man who she'd even think about approaching at the moment . . . or was Jake not what she thought too? Was she that bad of a judge of character?

She dropped onto her back and stared up at the ceiling for a while, listening to Matt babble incoherently, wishing he was speaking English so she could understand some of what he was saying, even a little bit. She wondered how much of their life together had been a lie. Was he really an accountant? Did he really have his own accounting business in downtown Plymouth or was that a front? Was he, like, a numbers guy for the mob or something?

Did the mob employ accountants in the 'burbs?

As she lay there next to the blood stain that was growing and morphing and taking on a life of its own, she felt the energy slowly return to her body. The red blood stain filled out, like an inflated balloon. Head, neck, arms, chest and stomach, legs, until she was looking at a red, fluid three-dimensional image of herself. It was yucky and fascinating at the same time.

It sat up all on its own and Matt, who could obviously see it, shrunk back in terror, squealed like a stuck pig, and then dropped in a dead faint. Then the red blob turned around and flew into the air. It landed smack-dab on top of her, then sunk in.

Oh . . . that was a unique sensation. Very erotic. Heat spread out from her belly to her fingers and toes, pulsing, while her heart pounded out a steady lub-dub in her ears. Her breathing sawed in and out of her chest and a very nice tingle settled between her legs. The tingling built until her muscles were all knotted and trembling. But she didn't receive release.

Finally, frustrated, hornier than a dog in heat, she sat up. She felt alive and refreshed and revitalized without the benefit of orgasm. Hopefully she'd get that soon enough too.

She climbed from the bed, stepped over the still-unconscious man lying on the carpet, and stared at him for a split second. The blood that had been all over his hands, face, and chest was gone. The blood in the bed was gone too.

"That was freakin' crazy," she said, then stepped over him and left, turning the corner and heading back to Jake and rehearsing her plea for his help.

She'd have to explain to him she was dead. How the heck did you tell that to the man you've spent the past twenty-four hours having sex with?

"Hello, honey, I'm home. Oh, and by the way, you've

been boning a dead girl for the past twenty-four hours. Now you want to help me figure out who murdered me?"

Well, she supposed that would work as well as any other lame explanation would.

She shuddered, still upset from the shocking news she'd just received. Maybe she could wait just a little while, like a couple of hours. She needed some comfort, some TLC, some hugs . . . and kisses . . . and strokes . . . and bites. . . .

Then she'd break the news to him, after she felt a little less shaken. Yeah. Was she a selfish wench for wanting some comfort? Surely he'd understand after she told him. Then again, maybe it was better if she told him she was dead before they made love again. Otherwise, it might just creep him out.

Determined to fess up and take the chance that he'd bolt, even if it meant she wouldn't enjoy the benefit of his strong, reassuring embrace, she hurried back to the apartment.

She climbed the stairs two at a time, sucked in a deep breath in preparation for her long-winded explanation, and charged through the door. "I have to tell you something."

The second she walked inside, Jake grabbed her in a tight bear hug and lowered his head to kiss her.

"Wait, I have to tell you . . . mfrghhhh . . ."

His tongue sliding into her mouth took all hope of her explaining, at least for the moment, and threw it right out the window.

She wasn't complaining.

Quite pleased with his idea of a welcome home, she lifted her hands to his shoulders and clung to him, pressing her pelvis into his leg and relishing the warmth coming off his body. Rather belatedly, she realized she'd been cold.

As was to be expected, his kiss was thorough and intoxicating. He tasted sweet and smelled even better. His lips worked over hers, smooth as satin, and his tongue dipped in and out of her mouth, probing, tasting.

A moment later, he was pulling her into the bedroom and coaxing her to lie down. He helped her out of every stitch of clothing, starting at her shoes and working his way up, until she was completely nude. And then, being diplomatic, she did the same for him. They tumbled onto the bed, wrapped in each other's arms, rolling over and over, like entwined fallen logs on a river. Then he settled between her thighs and without preamble—so unlike him—thrust inside.

Not quite ready, she huffed a surprised, "Oh!" but as he drew out slowly, then slid back in, her next utterance was more of a low, throaty "Ohhhh . . ."

"I'm sorry, baby. I'm so sorry," he muttered in her ear, then to her neck and breast and shoulder as he kissed every part of her upper body he could reach while gliding that rigid rod in and out of her body. "Next time I'll go slow. Promise."

Who was complaining? She tipped her pelvis and his groin rubbed delightfully against her with each forward thrust, creating instant heat. She felt it building with each stroke, each kiss, each thrust until she was riding the crest of a delightful climax.

He groaned in her ear and slowed his pace, which she was grateful for as she spasmed around him. She felt the increasing slickness of her own juices combined with his as he continued thrusting even after he'd come. Finally, when they were both worn out completely, he stopped and rested his weight on top of her.

Smiling, she wrapped her legs around his waist, trapping him where he was.

"I'm sorry, baby," he whispered to her collarbone, between heavy breaths.

"Sorry for what? You have something to tell me?"

"I'm sorry for going so fast. I know you deserve better. I promise next time. I couldn't help myself. I missed you."

"Hush. I missed you too. And I'm glad you made love to me, quickie or not. Now rest. Tomorrow's going to be a big day. I have something important to tell you and then we're going to . . ." When she heard the faint buzz of a snore, she stopped. No sense talking to a guy who was not quite literally dead to the world. She'd explain her dilemma tomorrow. That was probably better then.

Hopefully, he had a stomach for shocking news in the morning. If not, who knew how ugly things could get.

"I have something to tell you," they both said as they sat at the table for breakfast.

"You go ahead," Claire offered, worried by his proclamation and not in such a big hurry to drop her bomb.

"No, ladies first. I insist."

"You would say that. Gotta be a gentleman to the bitter end." She grinned, letting him know she was teasing. She sighed and tried to clear her head. A million different ways to say the unbelievable were bouncing around in her mind, all at one time. Kind of like those lottery number balls or a roomful of super balls.

He gave her an encouraging nod, then sipped his coffee and set it down, his gaze never once straying from her face.

"This is hard to explain. I . . . uh . . . don't suppose you believe in the afterlife?"

"Oh, yes. Absolutely. I sure do."

Well, that would make things a smidge easier, she hoped. "Good. Well . . ." She felt a lump of nerves clog her throat and emptied her glass of orange juice in one giant swallow. She set the glass on the table. "I don't know how to say this."

"Please, don't be afraid I'll be mad or freak out or anything. I swear I won't."

"Thanks." She sucked in a final deep breath, then blurted out, "Then I'll be blunt. I'm dead. Died nine years ago and I'm only here on earth for nine days and nights and then I have to go back and—"

His eyes widened with surprise, disbelief, maybe . . . ? Was he having a heart attack? Or a shock-induced aneurism? "You're what?"

"Now, before you call the guys with the Love-Me coats, let me explain."

"You're a Spirit American," he said.

"Huh?" To her knowledge no living human knew about their politically correct designation. "How'd you know about that? Nobody knows about that except for . . . other . . . Spirit Americans." Shoot! She really was blind when it came to people! She hadn't even realized Jake here was dead! She wondered what else she'd missed.

He nodded.

"So that's why you don't have a car. Or money. Or a house. Doesn't that just suck the way they throw you down here with nothing and then expect you to make your own way? They don't even give you a freaking credit card."

He chuckled.

"When did you . . . you know?"

"From the sounds of it, shortly before you did, maybe even the same day. You?" he asked.

"Wednesday night, September 6, 1995."

"Same week, same year, different day. I went Thursday morning."

"Damn." Lightheaded from shock for the second time in twenty-four hours, she gripped the edge of the table and tried to will her racing, stuttering heartbeat back into a life-sustaining pace and rhythm. "How?"

"Motor vehicle versus train. The train won."

"Your Hummer?"

He nodded. "A steel pancake. There's at least one thing

a Hummer can't stand up against—a train doing an impersonation of a rolling log, for one."

She smacked herself in the forehead. "Oh no! And I made that smart-alecky comment about your hair looking too good for you to have been run over by a train. I'm sorry. What a stupid thing to say."

"Not a problem. You didn't know. Actually, I considered it a compliment." He took her hand away from her head and gently held her fingertips in his. "What about you? How did you pass away? Please tell me it was gentle, painless."

"Depends upon how you define gentle," she murmured.

"Darn it!" He slammed his palm on the table, making her jump. Then, more softly, "Tell me. Please."

"I will if you promise not to do anything rash."

"I promise."

"I . . . was . . . shot." Her gaze fixed on his eyes, she saw the flash of rage shoot through them.

"Shot," he whispered, his soft tone belying the anger she saw in the tense lines of his jaw and neck. "By whom? I'll kill the bastard. Just tell me who it was."

"I'm a little afraid to."

He nodded and visibly relaxed his face, neck, and shoulders. She watched the tension drop away from them right before her eyes but in his eyes the rage still simmered. "I swear I'll behave myself."

"Oka-a-ay," she said, not sure if she should tell him the truth or not. "This is the deal. I'm not sure what happened. When I . . . you know . . . I thought the men were burglars. My fiancé kept a lot—and I mean a lot!—of money squirreled away in his house. He claimed he didn't trust banks to keep it safe."

"Ha!"

"Yeah, that's what I say now. I was an idiot back then to believe him. I'm realizing I'm not the brightest bulb in the box when it comes to men—nothing against you. Anyway, last night when I went back there—"

"You went there?"

"I died in my nightie. You've gotta realize that by now. Remember what I was wearing when we first bumped into each other at the bar?"

"Oh. Yeah. How could I forget?" His face gained a slightly red tint. He cleared his throat.

"So, I went back there and he couldn't see me but there was all this blood all over the bed and the jerk-off freaked out and pissed his pants and then said he was sorry for what happened."

"Hmm . . ." One hand on his jaw, he visibly digested what she'd told him. Finally he said, "He could've meant he was sorry about the burglars."

"He said if he'd known what they were going to do to me he never would've . . . um . . ." How exactly had that gone? "Darn it. I can't remember his exact words. But I got the impression he knew the guys and he knew something was up."

He shook his head. "Shit. I saw him with you years ago. Knew he didn't love you like I thought you deserved to be loved. But I never thought. Never. Shit," he repeated over and over.

"Now I want to know the truth. I need to know the truth. It was my death. It ended my life, my chances to finish college, go to France . . . have children." She felt her nose burning, which meant she could very well start bawling if she didn't change the subject quickly. "I don't know how to find it. And I need someone's help . . . Someone who won't think I'm nuts. Will you help me?"

"Yes, but I am—er, I was—a doctor, not a detective. How will I help you?"

"Well, at least you believe me when I say I'm dead. That right there is a huge head start. So, what do you say?

Want to help me find out the truth about how I died? Please?" When he didn't answer, she added, "I have no one else to ask. And I don't expect you to go chasing around town wearing tweed and smoking a pipe or anything. I'll be happy if you just help me brainstorm."

He hesitated for a moment, then said, "Okay. It's the least I can do, considering . . ." He cleared his throat. "I'll help you as long as you don't expect me to do anything illegal."

"Yay! We can be like *Hart to Hart*."

"Who?"

"Never mind." She grabbed him and planted a kiss on his cute private-investigating lips.

Chapter 12

"Now that we've had our morning lovin', where do we start with our mystery?" Claire was cuddled up to Jake, naked as the day she was born, and still tingling all over from another thorough lovemaking session. Each time, Jake made it special, exploring different fantasies she hadn't known she'd had. Those fuzzy pink handcuffs had only been the start and now the place she'd dreaded most—the torture chamber, as she liked to call it—was more like heaven on earth than a place to fear. She was quite certain, recalling her college psychology classes, that there was a technical term for it. Positive reinforcement. Conditioning? Something like that.

If only she could stay there forever!

"I'm not trying to weasel out of anything, but are you sure you want to go through with this?" Jake kissed her shoulders, sending a blanket of goosebumps down her arm.

"Of course I'm sure."

"What if you find out something you didn't want to know, like your fiancé—"

"I learned he pisses his pants when he gets scared. You think I could learn anything more shocking?"

"You never know."

She tipped her head to look up at Jake's handsome face. She doubted she'd ever get tired of looking at it, at the slight cleft she hadn't noticed before in his chin, or the mole on his left cheek, just under his eye. "I hate Matt right now because he practically confessed to my murder, but I have to admit I feel a little sorry for him too. He looked pathetic, nothing like he used to. His clothes were ratty, his face wrinkled, his head bald. He cried like a sissy when he figured out it was me. I get the impression he's been feeling bad about this for a long time. Who knows, maybe I'll learn something that might make him feel better."

"Or worse."

"Yeah, maybe. I need to know for my own reasons too. I need to know I wasn't so wrong about him, that I wasn't so blind. I was with him five years. How could I not know he was a criminal? I don't know if I can trust my gut feeling about a man again until I get some answers."

"You can trust your gut instinct about me. You know that, don't you?"

She looked into his searching gaze. There was no chance she could tell him the truth but she didn't have the heart to lie to him either. Her only option left was avoidance. "Ah, so you are the womanizing control freak I thought you were," she joked.

"No. I'm not a womanizer. The control freak you got me on." He turned his head and sighed in mock shame.

"See? I'm a terrible judge of character," she said, playing along, grateful to him for not pressing the issue.

"I was joking." He turned to face her again. "Look, you and I both know our time here is limited." He stroked her arm and lifted his eyebrows as he spoke and she knew what he was getting at.

"True. But honestly, do you think we're supposed to spend our time here just fooling around like a couple of horny teenagers? Doesn't that sound a bit . . . hedonistic?"

"We both paid our dues or we wouldn't still be here. You did your good deed. I did mine. That's all we were required to do."

"Sure. But I'd like to think we're here for another reason. Something greater."

"It's too dangerous. Besides, you've been watching too many movies."

"I had a lot of catching up to do," she admitted sheepishly. "Hey, I've only watched two so far. *Braveheart* and *The Pirates of the Caribbean* were on cable last night. I couldn't sleep after . . . you know. I needed something to distract me for a while."

"And my thorough, earth-rocking lovemaking didn't provide enough of a distraction?" he asked boastfully.

"You were dead to the world after a ten-minute quickie," she stated without apology.

"Oh. Yeah. I was a little worn out. But I made up for it this morning, didn't I?"

"You bet." She sighed and stretched. "But now we're going to get our lazy butts out of bed, shower, get dressed, and hit the road, in search of answers . . . as soon as I figure out where we should look first."

"Well, if you don't mind, while you're thinking, I'll just be over here snacking." He nipped her neck, then shoulder, and his warm hand closed over her breast. His thumb and forefinger found her nipple and pinched, then pulled gently.

Oh, that little sneak! She knew what he was up to . . . and it was working. She giggled and shrugged her shoulder, hoping to keep him from doing any more damage to her willpower. Her neck was definitely a weak spot. It seemed like the nerves there led straight to her nether parts.

Undaunted, he scooted lower, replacing his fingers with his warm, moist mouth, and despite the fact that they'd made love less than an hour ago, she was ready to go again.

She closed her eyes and said, “You’re naughty.”

“Are you complaining?” he asked between licks and nips.

“No.”

“Good. Then hush up and enjoy,” he teased. “I’ve only got seven days and nights left to show you all the pleasure I can. I need to make each minute count.” He kissed one breast, sucking gently while kneading the other. “No time for small talk.”

“Yeah . . . no time . . .” she murmured, well on her way to bliss.

“So what do you say about trying the swing this time?”

“Swing?” she repeated as she felt his hand inching lower, into the nest of curls between her legs. “Don’t you think we’re a little old to be playing on swings?”

“Not that kind.” He chuckled and she forced her heavy eyelids to lift. “That kind.” He pointed at the chair suspended from the ceiling in the corner of the room.

“Oh. I thought that was some kind of fancy chair. You know. Like the ones they sell at the Renaissance Festival every year. I just love those things. They’re so comfortable. . . .” She let him help her sit, then stand, and followed him as he took her hands in his and back-stepped toward the swing. “But that one doesn’t look so comfy. How the heck do you sit in it? Where’s the seat part? Is it maybe missing some pieces?”

“Oh no. Everything’s here. Believe me.” He turned her around and helped her lean back until one of the straps was positioned across the lower part of her shoulder blades. “First you lean like this.” He whispered into her ear, so close she could feel the heat coming off his body. Unable to resist, she tipped her head forward and stuck her tongue in his ear, which made him flinch and chuckle. It was a nice result, all the way around.

"Now, you stop that," he scolded, not exactly sounding like he meant it. "Cooperate with me here."

"I am cooperating. I couldn't help it if your ear got in the way."

"Of your tongue?" he asked.

"It needed some air?"

"Cute." He reached down and stroked her kitty and she just about melted.

"Cute? Remember, I don't care for that adjective. Could you please pick another?"

"Keep behaving like this and I'll have to spank you."

She grinned. "Promise?"

"Oh heck," he said, shaking his head. "Could you at least pretend to be a little scared?"

"I suppose. Here, let me see if this is better." She thought for a moment then said, "Oh, please, master. I promise I'll be a good slave girl. Please don't strike my round, soft bottom with that wonderful little flogger again." She checked his face for a reaction and, pleased with what she saw—red cheeks and ears—she asked, "Better?"

"Yeah." He pulled another strap down under her bottom. "There. Now lean back and let the swing hold your weight."

She lifted her feet off the ground. "Oh. This is kind of fun." She started rocking back and forth, hoping to gain some momentum.

"Okay. That's enough of that. You're not supposed to take flight." One arm on either side, his body smack dab in front of her, he caught the straps going up toward the ceiling in each of his fists and brought her motion to a halt. Quick. And that's when she realized how handy that swing might be. Her bottom was positioned at exactly the right height for him to love the daylights out of her.

"Drats," she said, not sounding the least bit disappointed, even to herself.

"Now, give me your leg," he coaxed.

She lifted one knee and watched as he secured it in a very open position with one strap, then gave him the other. Wow. To say she was no longer feeling like goofing off was an understatement. Seeing him look at her with eyes full of fierce hunger was doing all kinds of crazy things to several parts of her body, in particular her sex. Her heart too. It sounded like her old Pinto when it used to chug and backfire after she shut it off.

"How do you feel?" he asked, running a fingertip down one thigh, then up again.

Now, that was a silly question! "Um . . . warm."

"That's a good start." He leaned in close and nibbled her neck, adding chills and goosebumps to the mix. His left hand cupped her breast while his right dropped to the juncture of her thighs.

She swallowed a lump the size of a small mountain. "Good start?"

"I promised I'd take things slow from now on. And I aim to keep that promise."

She felt her temperature rising with each probing touch between her legs and with each squeeze of her breast. Surely if this continued much longer she'd combust. "How slow?"

"Really slow." His finger dipped between her slick folds and she groaned and let her eyelids fall closed.

"Oh . . ."

"Open your eyes for me. Don't close me out already."

It took a lot of effort to open them but she did it.

"Let's see if I'm a decent judge of character," he murmured with his husky sex voice. "I think this is the way you've always wanted to be, isn't it?"

"Tied up?"

"No, but completely under the control of your man." He traced small circles around her nipple.

"Not exactly, but I'm not complaining either."

"To be open to him, physically, emotionally." He stroked her burning flesh and she bit back a groan. He truly knew how to push her buttons.

"Um . . ." What had he asked her?

His fingernail scraped against her sensitive bud and she practically yelped in glee. "Look at you. So perfect." He pushed two fingers inside.

"Oh . . ." Her passage muscles clenched around his probing fingers, increasing the friction as he slowly drew them out, then pushed them back in.

"So wet and sweet." He lowered his head and parted her folds with his free hand while he continued to slowly thrust in and draw out those wonderful fingers. With a quick swipe of his tongue, he increased the temperature in the room by at least a hundred degrees.

She felt droplets of moisture collecting along her upper lip and squirmed. The muscles in her legs and stomach coiled tight like springs.

His tongue flickered over her nub, sending little bursts of pleasure up her spine. Lacking the strength to hold it up any longer, she let her head fall back and caught the straps next to her shoulders in her fists. "Oh yes," she muttered over and over as she felt the trembling flush of orgasm spreading over her body.

"Don't come yet." He stopped teasing her and stepped away, returning a few seconds later. "Look at me. Now."

Darn it! What was with this open your eyes stuff? It wasn't natural. She lifted her head and opened her eyes again, just in time to watch him push a giant dildo into her sex. She gasped, her inner walls instantly clasping the cool piece of plastic as it slid deep inside.

"That's it. Oh yes." He drew it out, then pushed it back in. "Watch it."

She looked down. Wow, what a sight, that huge dildo, wet and sleek, sliding in and out of her.

He licked his lips and watched, his hot gaze fixed on one spot. His cheeks stained a deep red. "Damn it, I'm going to come just watching this."

"You and me both."

He left the dildo deep inside her and reached down to pick up a tube of jelly. "Can I touch your bottom?"

"Yes."

He covered his fingertip with the transparent gel, then, leaving the dildo where it was, teased her tight entry.

Instinctively, she tensed the muscle, resisting his entry.

"Relax, baby. I promise I won't hurt you. You'll love this. I promise."

She nodded and tried to concentrate on opening to him. His finger pushed against her delicate tissues. It burned a little, but not enough to make her cry out. It was a good burn. A sexy burn. Then it slid inside and she moaned.

What a feeling! Her sex full, her bottom full. Oh . . .

"That's the way. Yes." He pushed his finger deeper and anxious for more. More in her sex, more in her bottom, she drew her legs back farther. "Yes. Open to me. That's the way."

The world was spinning away as she soared upon wave after wave of pleasure. Hot and wet and pulsing, it carried her closer to completion until she was panting hard, trembling all over and at the very limit of her control. Sensations blended and intensified, even as she closed her eyes to shut some of them out. She tasted sounds and felt colors. She couldn't take any more. "I want to come," she moaned.

"No. Not yet." He slowly pulled his finger out and she felt the orgasm that had been quickly approaching fade away.

"Meanie!"

"Watch me. Watch what I'm going to do." He withdrew the dildo and nuzzled his pelvis between her legs and slowly, inch by delectable inch, buried his thick erection in her.

Watching almost made her come, just like that.

"Oh, God," she said, looking up at his face.

Signs of tension spread over his face, neck, and shoulders. As he pulled her toward him then pushed her away, his biceps bulged, then relaxed. His shoulders became fuller as they worked, making her sex throb. "That's it, baby. Damn it, you're so hot."

"Yeah . . ."

His fingers dug into her hips, adding another delightful sensation to the myriad already threatening to overwhelm her system once more. His pelvis made a delightful slapping sound as it smacked against her with each thrust and the scent of man and sex filled the air, making her head swim.

He pushed her legs out to the sides, which made the angle of his thrusts change oh-so-slightly. But the effects were more than slight. She was trembling all over now, her blood flying through her body, pushed through by a heart that was thudding heavily against her ribcage.

"Now, touch yourself."

"What?"

"Touch yourself. Do it for me, love. I want to watch. And don't close your eyes. I want you to see how turned on I am."

She stared at his amazing chest as she reached a trembling hand down to her folds, and the instant her finger made contact with her nub, she saw his pecs tighten into two firm planes.

"Oh, yeah."

She reached her other hand down and parted her wet lips for him, then drew slow, rhythmic circles over her nub. One, two, three, in time with his deep thrusts. The combination of sensations, of sounds and scents and sights, was more than she could handle. She needed release. She needed it now.

"That's it. You can come for me. Do it now, baby."

As if her body had been waiting for his permission, it

took over, succumbing to a powerful orgasm that quaked her to the soul. She cried out, reaching forward and raking her fingernails down his arms. Her shouts were joined by his as he too found release, pumping his seed into her spasming sex. He thrust and thrust until her last spasm. And then, visibly spent, his shoulders droopy and his arms loose and floppy, he released her from the straps and helped her stand. Her legs felt wobbly and soft, like half-molten marshmallows. Afraid she might fall, she made a beeline for the bed and lay down.

Flat on her back, Jake at her side, she rested until her breathing had slowed and it felt like she had bones in her body again. "Wow. That was . . . wow."

"Wow as in good?"

"Wow as in amazing. I never knew it could be like this."

"What?"

"Sex. I mean, it was okay with Matt. But not . . . not even close to like this. Wow."

"Oh yeah?" He rolled onto his side, bent his arm, and propped his head on his upturned palm. "What was the best part?"

"What part wasn't?"

"Seriously." He traced her collarbone with an index finger. "Tell me so I know what I'm doing right."

"You're doing everything right. Absolutely everything." She rolled onto her side and wrapped an arm around his neck. Her eyes closed, her cheek pressed against his chest, she listened to the slow, steady thump of his heart for a while. He didn't press her for more, which she was thankful for, so she just wallowed in after-sex bliss for a while. But unfortunately, she couldn't allow herself to do that for too long. Now clear of the fog that had muddled her brain while they were making love, her mind was beginning to wander.

So many questions. So little time.

Her body still not one hundred percent back to normal, she sat up.

"Where are you going?"

"We have a mystery to solve, remember?"

He groaned. "Can't it wait until tomorrow? I'm tired. You know what sex does to a guy."

"Yeah, yeah. I've heard it all before. Up you go. Maybe a shower will get you going." She caught his big hands and pulled. He didn't budge. It was like trying to pull a ten-ton hunk of steel from the bed.

"A half hour. Just give me thirty minutes to close my eyes," he pleaded.

"Fine." He looked so delicious laying there naked, the sheet thrown across his hips, and smelled so amazing, she was tempted to climb right back in there and forget all about her mystery. But she convinced herself not to. A promise of chocolate helped.

She took a quick shower, then dressed, helped herself to some ice cream from John's freezer, and settled in front of the computer.

The Internet seemed a logical place to start. She tried the two largest newspapers first but found nothing. "Hey, I died! Was shot in my own freaking bed and I don't rate a story in the *Detroit News*?" she grumbled. Next, she tried a couple of smaller papers. She found a short clip in the *Observer. Girlfriend Shot by Fiancé in Gun Accident.*

"Huh? That's not what happened." She read farther.

Claire Weiss of Plymouth was fatally wounded when her fiancé accidentally discharged his gun while cleaning it. No arrests were made and no further investigation is planned.

Why would Matt lie? Why wouldn't he tell someone—the police, the newspapers, anyone—about the burglars?

What the heck happened? Had he been threatened not to tell?

Angry and frustrated, she turned off the screen and went in the bedroom to see if Jake was up yet.

She noted that fortunately he had already showered and dressed from the waist down. He took one look at her face and crossed the room in three long strides to gather her into his arms. He smoothed her hair with his hand. "What's wrong?"

"He lied to the authorities or someone is covering up the truth," she said to his chest. "I looked on the Internet. The only article I found said I was accidentally shot by Matt when he was cleaning his gun. He never owned a gun. What's going on here?"

"I don't know, babe. But we'll find out."

She blinked away an eyeballfull of hot tears. But that just made the annoying wetness run down her cheek. Crying sucked. It was messy, produced the most God-awful byproducts, such as mucus, and gave her a headache. She refused to cry. "I hope so."

He thumbed away a droplet that was hanging, like a fat raindrop on a twig, from her chin. "We won't stop looking until we find out what we want to know. Now, please don't cry."

"I'm not . . ." she sniffled, snorted, and blubbered, "crying."

He chuckled and palmed her cheek. "Oh. Okay."

"The wetness is from allergies. I'm allergic to . . . to murder. Yeah. And crooked cops and lying fiancés."

"I think anybody would be. Come on. Let's go." Obviously ignoring the fact that she was barefoot, he took her hand and led her toward the front door.

"Where are we going?" she asked.

"To your fiancé's house." He sort of spat out the *f*- word, not that she blamed him. Even if they were only bed pals for nine days, it still had to be tough for him to deal with this. How awkward, being caught in the middle of this mess between her and her ex. Come to think of it, Claire admitted, she probably wouldn't handle it near as well as he was.

"This must be kind of yucky for you. I hadn't thought about it until now. If you want to back out, I completely understand."

"Heck no." He caught her shoulders in his huge hands and looked down at her with stern eyes. "I would never make you do this by yourself. I'm no detective or anything, and I have no idea if I'll actually be much help, but I'd be a world-class jerk if I just threw you out there by yourself to try to figure this out."

"Thank you." She smiled, even though she felt like bawling like a baby. "But one thing before we leave."

"What's that?"

"I need some shoes. Don't think they'd let me on the bus without them."

"There aren't any busses in Plymouth."

"And your point is?"

"Go get your shoes on and let's go ask that ex-fiancé," he said, emphasizing the "ex" part, "a few questions. I'm sure he'll be overjoyed to see you again." He chuckled.

Whew, that was one wicked laugh. She wouldn't want to be in Matt's shoes right now.

Chapter 13

"This place has always given me the willies," Claire said as they walked up the brick path leading to the office of Gerald and Murdock, CPAs. Housed in an old three-storey Victorian that could be the cover house for *The Amityville Horror*, the office had always been cold and creepy. She could count on one hand the number of times she'd visited Matt there.

"Doesn't look like such a bad place to me."

"You know, they say this old dump is haunted. Back in the 1940s and 50s it used to be a hospital, and one of the two sisters who used to run it is supposed to still be hanging around, knocking over Christmas trees and rearranging furniture."

"Well, I'll keep you safe." He wrapped a thick arm around her shoulders and gave them a gentle squeeze. "No dead Christmas-tree hater is going to hurt you."

"Oh, you're my hero," she teased, batting her eyelashes as she brushed past him to climb the stairs to the wide porch. "You'll beat up that nasty old ghost for me?"

"You bet." He opened the front door and held it for her and she stepped inside.

Immediately, the musty odor of old house filled her nostrils and she sneezed. Her eyes watered. Her nose tickled and she had to blink to see.

Through the tears, she noticed Barb, the receptionist sitting at the front desk, wearing the dress she'd had on the last time Claire had been to Matt's office. Evidently the woman couldn't care less about fashion trends.

Barb looked up from the papers she was working on and gave Claire a friendly smile. "Hello, Claire. It's been a long, long time. I'm so glad to see you."

A little relieved to see a familiar face, Claire felt some of the tension slip from her neck. She hadn't realized how stiff it had become. "Hi, Barb. It's good to see you too. How've you been?"

"Just fine, dear. How can I help you?" the older woman asked.

"Is Matt here?" Claire asked.

Barb gave Jake a quick assessing glance, then returned her attention to Claire. "Why, no. He called in sick today."

"Oh. Sick?"

"If he calls in for messages I can let him know you were here."

"No, that's probably not a good idea. Thanks anyway." Claire glanced up at Jake, then headed for the door. Before she left, she said, "What about Ben? I haven't seen him in ages. I'd love to say hello."

"He's away on a personal trip. Won't be back until the middle of next week."

"Oh, that's too bad. Oh well. It's good to see you again, Barb."

"You too, dear. You take care."

"You too." Claire walked back outside into the crisp, dust-free fall air and drew in a long, deep breath. The air smelled like fallen leaves and approaching winter. Yum. "Well, so much for talking to Matt."

"At least we didn't run into any scary ghosts."

"No, we didn't. Though I wonder, because we're Spirit

Americans, do you think we'd see them? They might even look like real people. How would we know the difference, I wonder?"

"I don't know. I haven't seen any ghosts that I know of." He took her hand in his as they strolled down the leaf-strewn sidewalk. "Why?"

"I was just thinking out loud." She looked at the shop windows as she passed them.

"Since we couldn't talk to Matt here do you want to go up to his home now?"

She glanced up at Jake's face. "No. I have to go there later anyway since, well, you know. Hopefully tonight he'll be able to see me. I wonder why he couldn't last night? Everyone else has been able to."

His brows furrowed. "I don't understand that either. Maybe it was because you had to recharge," he suggested.

"I guess that makes sense. There's so little I understand about all this stuff. They should write a manual, call it something like *Reanimating for Dummies*."

"Yeah. I'd read that one for sure and I'm a guy. We never read owner's manuals or assembly directions. Don't need to."

She laughed. "Let me guess—you never stop to get directions when you're lost either, do you?"

"Nope. Never. 'Cause I never get lost," he stated proudly.

"Yeaaaah, right."

He touched her nose with an index finger and smiled, and if it hadn't been so blasted chilly outside she might've melted right there on the sidewalk. When Jake Faron smiled, the angels had to sing in heaven. Okay, maybe not. But a Jake smile was a lovely sight. The whole world seemed brighter.

"By the way," Jake asked, "who's Ben?"

"Matt's partner. Really sweet guy. We used to go out together sometimes. Ben's married, or at least he was, so you have nothing to worry about." She gave him a teasing grin. "Ben's wife is a total babe—or was. Who knows anymore. Nine years can be hard on a woman, especially if she's popping out babies every year and a half or so. I'd be willing to bet they're up to ten by now."

"Ten kids?"

"They had four when I passed. They were almost half way there."

"Wow."

"Catholics, you know. Don't believe in birth control."

"Oh." He nodded with understanding.

They walked past a Thai-food restaurant and Claire insisted they run in and grab some food to eat at home. She got her usual, vegetable curry with coconut milk. Yum! He merely wrinkled his nose in silent disgust and waited patiently by her side for the food to be prepared.

She inhaled the scent as they walked.

Jake, who bought a sandwich from a deli a few doors down, carried their meals. His free arm rested possessively on her shoulder and she didn't mind a bit.

After they got home, gathered their drinks, and settled down to eat, Claire asked, "If I can't get any more information from Matt, what do you think we should do?"

"I'm not sure. I'm a neurologist, not a detective. I'm outta my element here."

"Okay. But if you were trying to solve a medical mystery, how would you approach it?"

"I'd ask the patient questions about their symptoms, then run some tests—EEG, MRI, whatever—until I could find a diagnosis."

"Hmmm . . . an MRI or EEG won't help me," she admitted before taking a bite of her meal.

"At least not in solving this mystery."

She laughed, just about spewing rice and baby carrots all over Jake's face. "Are you trying to say I have brain damage or something?"

All nonchalant, he popped a potato chip into his mouth,

chewed, and swallowed. "No . . . although now that you mention EEG's—"

"Actually, you mentioned them first."

"—it would be interesting to see what kind of brainwaves an EEG would pick up from a reanimated body."

"Oh boy, the man's getting all scientific on me," she teased before refilling her mouth with more rice and veggies.

"Sorry. Can't help it."

She swallowed and grinned. "Can't you put that brilliant mind of yours to work on my problem?"

"I'm trying, babe. Honest. But I'm not a pro. Remind me, why aren't we hiring a professional? We have money."

"Because the minute I tell a detective I'm dead and I want him to investigate how I was killed, he'll probably die from laughing so hard. And then I'd be sent not just to blah purgatory but to hell. Being bored out of my skull for all eternity is bad enough; burning in the eternal lake of fire is a whole other thing."

"But you wouldn't have killed him on purpose."

She stabbed at a piece of eggplant and lifted it but didn't put it in her mouth. "True, but I know my story would cause the kind of shock that can be fatal in persons with heart conditions, so I'd still be somewhat guilty," she joked. "I'm not willing to take the chance."

"Poor sweetie. You don't like being laughed at, do you?"

"No. I admit I'm a little sensitive about being laughed at, since I was a kid and fell in gym class and all the kids saw my underwear and laughed. I can still hear their screechy little voices. It was so traumatic. . . ." She sniffled dramatically and poked the eggplant into her mouth.

"Liar." He polished off his sandwich with one big bite, then stood to take his empty plate into the kitchen.

"Yeah. You're much better at reading people than I am. I can't get anything by you." Carrying her own empty plate, she followed him into the tiny kitchen, rinsed her dish, and put it in the dishwasher.

As she was bent over, Jake grabbed her waist from behind and did the old bump and grind to her rear end. "How about we forget about your mystery for now, since there isn't anything we can do about it, and make love."

She giggled and wiggled her butt suggestively. "You have a one-track mind. At least I've figured out that much."

"How can I not when I have a beautiful woman like you as a roommate?"

"More flattery?"

"You said it would get me everywhere. I'll settle for bed."

She spun around and found herself nose to nipple with him. Her nose to his nipple. It was a very disconcerting, if not arousing, position to be in. "I hope you understand."

He pressed his hand to his chest and staggered back one step. "Oh! The boy's been shot down."

"Only for now, silly." She socked him in the belly, which elicited an exaggerated gasp and over-dramatized stage fall.

"Oh-h-h-h, my belly," he moaned. "I think you broke something."

Stepping over him, she said, "I never would've guessed you'd be such a goof."

He caught her ankle in a vise-like grip. "Goof? Or stud?"

"Oh, the stud part I had you pegged for."

"Smart woman. See? You're not such a bad judge of men." He released her leg and in a karate-type maneuver jumped upright.

"Wow. Impressive."

"Black belt," he said, his arms folded over his chest. He looked quite proud of himself. And manly. And adorable. She wanted to sigh but didn't, figuring it would only feed his already over-inflated ego.

"In which of the martial arts?"

"None. But I have a black leather belt on. Wanna see?" He lifted his shirt. "And I have black underwear on to match," he added, pulling the zipper down.

"Oh no. Not right now. It's October and we won't have daylight for long and I need to spend some of it gathering some evidence—fingerprints or whatever—instead of rolling around in bed with you."

"I might disagree with you—" When she shot him a not-so-serious warning slant, he amended his answer to, "Of course, sweet. We'll do what you want. So, where do you want to look for clues?"

The man was a genius, not to mention sweet, and a lot of fun to look at. At least she hoped she saw him for who he was. Another sigh rose up into her throat. "We need to figure out what the deal was with the money he had in his house, since it looks like that was what the bad guys were after."

He leaned slightly to the right, resting a shoulder on the wall. "How're you going to figure that out?"

"I need to get a look at his personal records. Those men knew about Matt's money. How had they known? He had hidden it from me for ages and I was sleeping with him. So, the fact that they knew about it has to mean something."

"Interesting." Jake nodded thoughtfully. He stroked his jaw with his thumb.

"Any ideas how they'd know?"

"Maybe they worked for the bank? Assuming, of course, it had been in the bank at one time and he'd withdrawn it."

"Could be."

"Or maybe he'd stolen it from them."

She considered that explanation but it seemed so unlikely she had a hard time accepting it as a possibility. "That one's a stretch."

"Okay, what if he stole it with them?"

"Like a bank heist?"

"You never know."

"If Matt got an extra bag of chips from a vending machine he'd put the money in an envelope and tape it to the back of the machine with a note. I can't imagine him being involved in anything illegal, let alone dangerous."

"Sounds like a real gem," Jake said sarcastically, pushing away from the wall and walking toward the couch.

"Hey, he might've been a lot of things, but he wasn't a bank robber . . . and he wasn't the love of my life," she admitted to his retreating back.

That confession shut Jake up for more than a handful of heartbeats, making her regret having said it. Finally, his back still to her, he spoke. "Back to your mystery. Let's try a different angle." He finally turned to face her and rested his rump on the couch armrest. "Do you remember what the men looked like?"

"Yes. That's the other thing. Now that I think about it, most burglars try to mask their identity somehow. But these men didn't. They were dressed like they'd just come out of a restaurant, or an office. Both were very large, bigger than you—and that's saying something. I don't remember what color their eyes were or what exactly they were wearing, though."

"Might not be significant."

She plopped onto the couch. "I hope I haven't forgotten an important detail."

"No way of knowing. Anything else stand out about them?" he asked.

"They said Matt's name. I remember that. Mentioned the money and said something about Matt having a big mouth. Do you think that's because he told someone about his savings?" she asked, looking up at him.

"Or maybe something else," Jake suggested, his eyes brightening.

"Oh-h-h . . . Like what?" She leaned closer, encouraging him to continue.

"I don't know. A secret someone didn't want to get out?"

Not following his line of thought, she asked, "What would that have to do with money?"

"They could've paid him money to keep his mouth shut and he blabbed anyway."

"Wow, you're good. Maybe I should be taking notes." Claire got up and rummaged through the nearby buffet, looking for a pencil and paper. Finding one, she sat down again and started scribbling notes. "That sounds more like Matt. He couldn't keep a secret for anything. Keep going. You're doing great. Are you sure you aren't lying about not being a detective?"

"I'm not lying, and that's all I've got."

"Okay. So . . ." She looked down at her notes. "What kind of secret would an accountant be expected to keep?"

"That seems pretty obvious."

"Money?"

"Yeah. The root of all evil."

"Actually, the love of money is the root of all evil," she corrected.

"Close enough," he said with a crooked grin.

"So, now we have a possible motive. Don't they say if you can find the motive, you'll find the culprit?" she asked, chewing on the pencil eraser.

"Something like that."

"Well, if he was keeping a secret involving money, it would likely be for one of his clients," she said, thinking out loud as she drew little boxes on her notes.

"Excellent assumption."

"Which means we need to go back to his office."

"Isn't it too late for that now? I mean, his receptionist must've gone home by now."

"Sure." She shrugged. "We'll have to break in."

"Wait a minute." He shot to his feet and scowled at her. "You promised me we wouldn't do anything illegal. Besides, isn't this all a bit premature? You could go over to his place tonight and he could tell you the whole story."

"True."

"Why take such a risk if you don't have to?" he asked, taking her hands in his. He pulled gently until she was standing too.

"Where are we going?"

"We have a couple of hours before we have to go back and recharge . . ." he winked suggestively.

"Again? My gosh! Don't you ever . . . er, run out?"

"Normally, yes. But I guess after nine years of abstinence, my body has built up some reserves."

It didn't take a whole lot of effort for him to get her into the bedroom.

Chapter 14

For some reason, a completely naked man dancing in the middle of the bedroom, his member wagging up and down like a dog's tail while he sang a bad rendition of "Let's Go All the Way," was not a mood enhancer. Instead, it induced an extremely persistent case of the giggles.

Claire giggled as Jake kissed her. She giggled as he undressed her. And she giggled as he led her to the kneeler-looking contraption that had two low cushions on either side and a higher one in the middle. He told her to kneel down and bend over.

Really. How could staring at the one part of her body she despised most be erotic?

Maybe he wanted a good laugh too?

"Mmmm . . . you have the finest rear end I've ever seen." He wasn't laughing.

"Guess you haven't seen too many bottoms, eh? Since you were a neurologist and all," she asked, positioning herself over the tall part so her stomach was resting on the padded cushion. She placed her hands on the lower cushion on the other side. Kinda comfy.

He ran his hands over her rear end. His touch was soft, like silk. "I've seen my share. But yours is soft and round and kissable. Mmmm . . ."

"You aren't going to kiss my butt . . . yet. I mean, you haven't made me mad. There's really no reason," she joked.

"There's plenty of reason."

"This is silly." She started to stand up, but a large hand between her shoulder blades encouraged her to stay put.

"I'm going to kiss it. And then I'm going to do even more to it. And take my word for it—you're going to love it."

Maybe it was the position she was in, pressing on a stomach full of food, but suddenly there was a very large lump in her throat. Oh, and the giggles had ceased. "Like what?" she asked in a small voice.

"Nothing you won't thoroughly enjoy," he promised, stepping away from her for a moment.

She glanced over her shoulder, watching him gather some things from the Little Closet of Horrors and return with an armload of things she couldn't name. "That's quite a collection you've got there."

"Oh, this'll just get us started. There's plenty more where this came from." He set the stuff down on the bed.

"Yikes." She recognized a few of the items, a tube of lubrication gel, the dildo they'd used earlier, the handcuffs.

He approached her with the two sets of pink fur-lined handcuffs. "My buddy paid good money for this bench. It's obviously custom-made." He closed a fur-lined ring around each of her wrists, then fastened the other ends to loops on the other side of the bench, down low by the floor. Now she couldn't lift her upper body at all. "With these loops here. This is great."

"Yeah," she said unenthusiastically, despite the tingles zipping up and down her spine. "Just great."

"Are you comfortable?"

"Yeah. Except for the fact that I ate too much and now I'm pressing on my bloated belly."

"I won't leave you this way for long."

"Okay."

"You trust me, don't you?"

"Sure . . ." she said, not entirely positive.

"Tell me at any time if you want me to stop and I will. I promise."

"Okay. Um, don't people who get into this stuff usually use a safe word?"

"We could do that, yes. What word do you want to use? Make sure it's something easy to say." He was kissing the small of her back, giving her shivers.

It was not easy to think when she was quaking and shaking. "Mmmm . . . How about 'Braveheart'?"

"You liked that movie, didn't you?"

"Yeah," she said, imagining Mel naked from the waist down. "It was a great movie."

"Okay. "Braveheart" it is." He reached for the stack of goodies behind them, but thanks to the handcuffs, she could no longer look back to see what he was doing. "Have you ever had it in the bottom?"

"Heck no!" Her untried anus puckered at the thought. "And I'm not going to today either, thank you very much."

"Not if you don't want to," he said in a soft, soothing, reassuring voice. He was back to stroking her bottom, touching, kneading, massaging. That was nice. Very nice. When he parted her cheeks, her sex clenched and a spray of warmth washed up her back. "I won't ever force you to do something you don't like. Okay?"

"Okay." She was practically squirming now, thanks to his gentle strokes up and down, up and down between her cheeks. His touches found her every sensitive part. She shuddered and dropped her head, letting it hang from her shoulders. Her hair tumbled over top, the ends brushing the cushion below.

"I have a small vibrator. It isn't much bigger than my finger. I want to put just the tip inside. Will you let me?"

She felt him smooth a heavy coating of gel over her

anus. Her sex throbbed at the thought of him pushing a vibrator deep into her tight hole. When it snapped on, humming in her ear, she turned her head. Small, pink, it didn't look too terribly painful. "Okay." Her voice sounded breathy and low, like she'd run a marathon or was the host of a late-night radio show.

"Just remember the safe word," he said as he ran the tip of the buzzing vibrator up and down her crack. He slowly pushed it into her sex first, sliding it in and out several times until she was wet and throbbing and aching. Then he slid it up toward her anus and pushed oh-so-gently. "Open, baby." A finger found her vagina and dipped inside and she couldn't help clamping her inner muscles tight around it. "No, open."

"I'm trying." She concentrated on relaxing, no easy task when the part in question was burning from the pressure of the vibrator on her delicate skin. Yet, even though it stung, the vibration was also intense and so stimulating, she wondered if she'd lose control the second it was inside.

A tiny bit found its way inside and her sphincter tightened around it, which intensified the vibrating. The tingling vibrations zapped through her whole bottom and the heat of a quickly building climax shot to her face. She gasped.

"That's it baby. Take more. Oh, yeah, this is so sexy."

She twisted her wrists, fighting the shackles holding her down as he pushed the vibrator deeper and deeper. When she was sure she could take no more, she felt the tip of his erection begging entry into her.

"Take me. That's it."

She relaxed for a split second, allowing him in, then tightened her muscles around him. Instantly, before he had withdrawn for a second thrust, she came. She quivered and shook all over. The sensation was too intense. She called out, "Braveheart!"

He drew out the vibrator and shut it off, then slowly pushed deep inside her again. She welcomed him with a hot, spasming embrace.

"Oh, yes," she called out.

He drove into her, over and over in a steady rhythm that sent her racing toward a second orgasm.

When he reached down and began stroking her nub, she lost control again and succumbed to a second body-quaking orgasm. He groaned, then quickened his pace until his thrusts were jerky and tight, and then, with a huff spilled his seed into her still-tingling canal.

Slick with sweat, he briefly leaned over her back, his stomach brushing against her bottom, and kissed her back. Then he pulled out, unfastened the handcuffs, and led her to the bed. The product of their lovemaking trickled warm and wet down the insides of her thighs as she walked. She lay down.

"Wait right there." He went to the bathroom and returned with a warm, damp washcloth. Gently, he cleaned her, then went to take the washcloth back to the bathroom.

He returned a couple of heartbeats later, set the alarm for eleven, and gathered her into his arms. A goofy, satisfied smile on her face, she fell asleep.

A strange voice woke her hours later. Startled, still not quite sure what was part of her dream and what was reality, she sat upright and blinked in the darkness.

"It's eleven-oh-three in the Motor City and the streets are clear. No accidents or delays—"

She reached across Jake and hit the first button on the clock, which shut up Mr. Radio. Jake grunted as she fell on top of his chest.

"Sorry," she whispered.

"'S okay. You going to shower?"

She could feel her thighs sticking together, despite his efforts to clean her up earlier, and she still smelled the musky odor of sex on her skin. "I better."

"I'll wait until you're done."

She ran to the bathroom and took a long, hot shower. It was wonderful. But as she stepped out, she had the same weary, weak sensation she felt the night before. Like a wind-up toy running low. No doubt about it, she needed to get to Matt's place pronto.

She flipped on the light, which elicited another grunt from Jake, and quickly dressed. By the time she was ready to leave, he was upright, still rumpled and sleepy and tempting. She kissed him. "Wish me luck."

"Good luck. And I mean that. I'd much rather spend the rest of our time here doing what we did a couple of hours ago than running around chasing murderers."

"I bet," she joked, then added, "Me too." She hurried out the door before she lost the strength to leave and dragged herself down the empty streets to Matt's house.

Finally, completely exhausted and sure if she had to walk another hundred yards she'd collapse, she knocked on his front door.

He didn't answer.

When she knocked again and still received no answer, she became a little worried. He'd called in sick. What if he was seriously ill? Sure, she'd been miffed at him last night for having a hand in her death, but now that she'd had time to think about it, she was fairly certain it wasn't like she'd first thought. For sure, the guy didn't deserve to suffer in his own vomit on the bathroom floor, too weak to call for help—if that was what had happened.

She had to admit, she tended to have an overactive imagination.

She tried the front door. Unlocked, as usual. Odd, though, since last night he'd locked it.

She walked inside, calling, "Matt? Are you in here? Is everything okay?"

He didn't answer. Then again, he hadn't been able to hear her last night anyway.

"Hello, Matt! I don't want to take you by surprise again. Would hate to see you mess up another pair of pajamas." She knocked on the wall as she walked. She went to his bedroom and checked the bed first. Empty.

Oh, this was weird. In the five years they'd dated, he never once stayed up past midnight, not even on New Year's Eve.

She checked the spare bedroom, which was converted into an office. No one in there either. The kitchen. Empty. The living room. Empty. The garage, basement. Empty, empty.

She felt really crappy now. Her head was spinning, her knees wobbly. She needed to get into that bedroom and re-energize or whatever it was called. Pronto. Then she'd solve the mystery of the missing Matt.

She staggered back to the bedroom and lay on the bed. That raunchy, spoiled-meat odor filled her nostrils and she gagged. Then she felt the wetness of the red blob land on her body. Her heart beat faster, her lungs filled with air, and her head cleared.

Much better. She sat up.

Now, to find out what had happened to Matt. Maybe he'd been so sick he had to go to the hospital.

She hoped that wasn't the case. How the heck would she get in to see him if he was in the hospital? She could just imagine it.

Nurse: "Hello, are you family?"

Claire: "No, but I was his fiancée . . . er, before I died."

Nope. That probably wouldn't fly.

She went to the answering machine sitting on the kitchen counter. The red light was blinking. Maybe his messages would give her a clue.

Oh, maybe he'd been called out of town for something? Man oh man, now was not the time for him to take a business trip to the other side of the country.

She hit the play button on the machine and a soft crackle issued from the speaker.

"Hi, this is Linda with the *Detroit News*—"

Fast forward.

"Hello, Mr. Gerald, my name is Andy and I represent a company that offers—"

Fast forward.

She fast-forwarded through at least three more sales solicitations. This guy was clearly on every sales list that existed. Sheesh! Finally, she found a message that helped her some.

"Hey, Matt!" came a familiar male voice. Ben! "I'm gone a few days and all hell breaks loose. What's this shit about you signing yourself into the psych ward at Riverside? Tell me it's a joke. You owe me tickets to the Wings game next weekend. Call me."

Matt signed himself into the mental ward of a hospital? Stable, sane, do-everything-the-same-every-day Matt?

Egads! She'd pushed a sane man over the brink!

Chapter 15

"Get up. We've got to go break into Matt's office," Claire announced the minute she stepped into Jake's dark bedroom. She poked his shoulder and he snorted. "You went and got reenergized, didn't you?" she asked.

"Yeah. But I'm still tired. It's,"—he lifted his head and blinked at the clock—"two o'clock in the morning. A Spirit American has to get some sleep sometime, you know."

"Yeah. But now's not the time. You can sleep later, during the day."

"I'm not a vampire."

"Yeah, yeah." She slapped his sheet-covered butt. "Please get up. Or I'll go by myself."

"I'm getting up." He sat up and ran his palms over his whisker-stubbled face. "So I take it this means Matt didn't sing like a canary when you saw him tonight?"

"I didn't see him. He wasn't there." She paced back and forth, anxious to get going. "He . . . I guess I really scared the crap out of him the other night. He checked himself into the hospital."

Jake laughed.

"That isn't funny! That's the second person I've sent to the hospital in three days."

"Who else?" He stood and stretched. What a sight.

Long muscular arms, wide shoulders, broad chest, tight abs. Yummy.

"The lady I was trying to help on Halloween."

"What'd you do to her?"

"Made her dislocate her shoulder when I jumped forward to catch her groceries. I seem to scare people real easily these days."

"Huh." He grabbed her and brushed his lips over hers. "Well, you don't scare me . . . except maybe when you've got a bad case of bed head. Yeah." He nodded and grinned. "That's a little scary, the way your hair goes this way and that." He used his hands to illustrate.

"Watch it!" She smacked at his hands. Smiling right back at him, she traced the lines of his pecs with her fingertips, then pressed her flat palms against them. "Or I'll show you what it means to be scary. Now, go shower and drink some coffee. I need you alert."

"Did you find anything at his place while you were there?" he asked over his shoulder as he walked toward the bathroom, adjusting his boxers in a typical woke-up-with-a-hard-on fashion.

She smacked her forehead. "Duh! Why didn't I do some snooping? I was already there. But I was so freaked out when I found out about him going to the hospital. All I could think about was getting the heck outta there. I'm a rotten detective."

He stepped into the bathroom but poked his head out to say, "All the more reason to rethink this suggestion of yours. What makes you so sure you'll find something at the office, anyway?"

"Gut instinct?"

He went into the bathroom but left the door open. Over the sound of fluid hitting fluid as he peed, he said, "But does it make sense? Think about it. He kept the money in his house. Wouldn't he keep any documents relating to any kind of illegal or immoral transaction at home too?"

She sat on the bed and hugged a pillow to her chest. It smelled like Jake. She inhaled deeply. "I don't know. His client list would be at his office. I figured that would be a good place to start."

The toilet flushed.

Jake returned to the room, a hand towel in his fists. He dried his hands, then tossed the towel onto the dresser. "Then let's try to get it the legal way first. We can go there tomorrow, during regular office hours. You know the receptionist. Maybe you can make up a story about him keeping something for you at the office. Would that be believable?" He sat next to her.

"I don't know. Maybe."

"You can ask if you can go into his office to locate it and then grab his client list. Does he keep it on a computer?"

"He didn't years ago, but who knows now."

"Might be worth checking, if you can't find a book." He gathered her hair into his fist, then smoothed it down her back. "So, what do you think?"

"I guess that's an okay plan."

"Good. Now, let's go back to bed. I want to hold you." He pulled her toward the bed and watched with hungry eyes as she undressed. But to her surprise, when she climbed under the covers, he merely gathered her close and caressed her shoulder until she fell asleep.

The next morning, Claire was up with the birds—well, the birds that hadn't flown south in search of warm weather and thawed earthworms. She showered, dressed, and wolfed down a bowl of Cocoa Puffs before Jake had even stirred. Again, she found herself prodding him to get up. The man was not the easiest person in the world to wake.

She paced the floor nervously as he got dressed and ate. And she was glad they had a couple of miles to walk when they left. It would help burn off some of the nervous energy winding her muscles into tight balls. Her stomach felt yucky too—heavy, like it was made of lead.

She should've skipped the cereal this morning.

When they arrived at Matt's office they found Barb sitting exactly where she'd been yesterday, at the front desk, hunched over a stack of papers. She glanced up and smiled. "Hello, Claire. So good to see you again."

"Hi, Barb," Claire said, trying to sound casual. "Is Matt in today?"

"No, I'm sorry. He's still ill. Can I help you with something?"

"Maybe you can." She quickly ran through the story she'd made up this morning while waiting for Jake to get moving. "Matt was working on some quarterly tax figures for me. Did he tell you I started my own business?"

Barb's brows scrunched together. "Why, no, he didn't."

"Yes. I started a . . . jewelry company. I make handcrafted jewelry. Would you like to see a catalog?" Claire offered, knowing Barb never wore jewelry.

"Maybe later. Thanks."

"Anyway, I asked Matt to help me out with the quarterly tax payments, forms, you know. I've never been any good with government stuff."

"I remember." Barb nodded. "He told me about the time you'd mistakenly applied for a new social security number under an alias."

"He told you about that? How embarrassing." Her cheeks warmed. "I lost my card. Those forms are not idiot proof," Claire explained, feeling a little defensive. She couldn't believe Matt had told Barb that. She wondered what else he'd told her.

Had he told Barb about the time when she'd stood in the movie theater, forgotten the seat flipped up, and fell on the floor when she'd tried to sit back down? Or when she assembled a set of cheap lamps she'd bought from the furniture store wrong and one caught fire when she turned it on?

Or when she got herself shot in his bed . . . No, he must not have told her that. And if he had, or if she'd read the newspaper article, Barb would be freaking out right now wondering how she was talking to a dead woman. She wondered what kind of story Matt had dished up to Barb, to explain her sudden disappearance. "Anyway," Claire added, "Is there any chance you could *please* locate those forms for me? They need to go in the mail today."

"Let me see what I can do." Barb gave Jake a polite smile and left the room.

Claire didn't say a word to Jake as they waited, afraid Barb might overhear their conversation and get more suspicious. As it was, it didn't look like she was completely sold on Claire's story.

Barb returned a few minutes later, empty-handed, as Claire had expected. Wouldn't that have been weird if she'd actually found something?

"I'm sorry," Barb said. "I didn't find anything for you. You'll have to return once he's back to work."

Claire pretended not to be too anxious, like she didn't know Matt would probably be in the hospital for weeks. "Okay. When will that be?"

"I'm not certain. Hopefully next week sometime."

"But that's too late. I'll have to pay a huge fine." Claire sat down. She didn't have to pretend to be stressed out. She ran her hand up over her forehead and combed her fingers through her hair. "Shoot! What'll I do? I can't afford to pay penalties and then the IRS'll throw me in jail. . . ."

"I'm sorry, dear. If there was more I could do, I would."

"Would you let me go look?" Claire asked.

"Oh, I don't think so." Barb said, looking regretful but firm. "No one but Mister Gerald and Mister Murdock are allowed in that office. Ever."

"I understand. But I was engaged to Matt once and he is out of the office for who knows how long—I hope it isn't anything serious—and this is sort of an emergency."

Barb looked nervously from Jake to Claire, then back to Jake again. "Will this gentleman be coming with you?"

"Absolutely not. I'll stay here in the lobby," Jake answered.

Barb looked at Claire again, and Claire concentrated on giving her the most innocent, compelling expression she could drum up with half her breakfast in her throat.

"Okay," Barb conceded. "I shouldn't be doing this but I'd hate to see you pay a penalty if you can avoid it. I'm sure Mr. Gerald will understand."

"Yes. I'm sure he will." Claire hurried past the front desk toward Matt's office. "I'll only be a few minutes," she called over her shoulder.

She didn't close the door completely, figuring if she did it would make Barb more suspicious. Then she set about a thorough search of his office, starting with his desk drawers first. Naturally, his office was in complete order, not a single scrap of paper out of place. Luckily, as she'd hoped, he hadn't given up his old system of keeping track of clients. The worn, well-used leather-bound book that held their names and other vital information was where he'd always kept it, in the unlocked top drawer.

Claire shoved it into her pants, then covered it with her bulky sweatshirt and tried the computer. It was locked with a password. No luck. She tried the filing cabinets, but with dozens of drawers to search and no time, she figured that was probably a waste of time.

Giving up, she carried a rolled up stack of blank paper in her fist and pasted on a triumphant grin. She glided through the door to the lobby. "Found them!"

"Wonderful. Where did you find them?"

"They'd fallen on the floor behind the credenza." Making

sure she was facing the wall, she made a show of shaking and dusting the pages off.

"Oh, dear. That was probably my fault."

"No harm done. They're just a little dusty." She gave them a final shake, then folded them. "The point is I have them and can mail them on time. Thanks for your help, Barb." She caught Jake's elbow as he stood. "Ready?"

"Sure."

"Take care. Good to see you again," Claire called over her shoulder as she tried not to hurry out the door too fast.

"Good to see you too," Barb answered just before the door closed.

Claire waited until they were at least two full blocks away and at least two Plymouth police cars had rolled by without stopping and slapping handcuffs on them both before she said, "I got the book."

"Great!"

"I'm just not sure what good it'll do us. I mean, there are hundreds of clients in there. Names, addresses, and phone numbers. That's about it. How will I know if I'm looking at something important?"

"I don't know. I guess you'll just have to trust that gut instinct of yours."

"You're not helping me. My gut instinct isn't always right." She nudged his side with an elbow.

"I told you I'm not a detective. I'm a doctor. Give me a neurological disorder to diagnose and I'll show you what I'm made of."

"You've showed me what you're made of already, and you didn't need a neurological disorder to diagnose to do it," she joked, feeling like a load the size of an elephant had been lifted from her shoulders, even though she was basically no closer to solving her mystery than she'd been when they'd left the house.

He laughed. "That's what I like to hear."

"Don't let it go to your head."

"I promise I won't. I'll always be the humble guy you fell in love with."

Shocked he'd said those words, she glanced up at his face. "What made you say that?"

"Gut instinct?" He smiled. When she didn't respond, he added, "Woman's intuition?"

"You're a guy."

"True, but I've been in touch with my feminine side. I've even tried quiche."

That got a laugh out of her, which cut the tension, and left her feeling a little less uncomfortable. The man was adorable, a wonderful lover, and an excellent sidekick. But love? After only a couple of days—even if they were intense? Impossible. She didn't know him well enough yet. Heck, she hadn't known Matt well enough after five years of dating.

Love took years to develop. Love was not the silly swoony sing-along-with-all-the-love-songs emotion most people thought it was. Love was serious. It was about commitment and sacrifice. And there was no way she was ready to say that word yet. She'd never used that word casually before she passed away. She certainly wasn't going to start now, just because her time with someone was short . . . and that someone had the most incredible eyes . . . and made her laugh even when she didn't feel like it . . . and made her want to tell all her secrets.

That wasn't as important as knowing a person's heart, soul, and spirit, trusting them without the slightest shadow of doubt.

What she felt was infatuation. Lust. Deep, deep liking. Yeah. That's what it was. Deeper-than-the-deepest-ocean liking, where those weird fish with the huge teeth and glow worms lived.

They stopped at a store to pick up some thinking-food—

chocolate pudding, chocolate candies, and chocolate ice cream—then went back to the apartment. The minute Claire walked through the door she found the nearest seat and started reading through each page of the book, starting with the *A*'s.

Alberta, Albright, Allen. One name, address, and phone number after another. Nothing stood out. She moved to the table and blindly spooned a mouthful of Moose Tracks ice cream—the store didn't carry Ben & Jerry's!—into her mouth as she continued through to the *M*'s. Marshall, Mardine, Marilow . . .

She didn't lift her head when she felt Jake's hands on her shoulders.

"How's it going?" He kissed her temple and, despite her frustration, she smiled.

"Terrible. What's wrong with putting red circles or stars or something around the evidence? Huh?"

"Nothing, sweet, if the guy wanted to go to prison."

"Yeah, yeah." She glanced up and grinned.

"Want more chocolate?" he asked, naked from the waist up. He held a bowl of something in his hand. His expression was one of wicked playfulness.

"What are you suggesting?"

"I think you look a little tense. How about taking a short break for a snack? It might help you see things in a whole new way." He lifted the spoon from the bowl and smeared brown pudding over his chest. "Oops. I'm such a clumsy oaf." He sighed.

Chapter 16

"That's chocolate abuse." Tsking at him, she stood, turned, and licked his yummy chest clean, taking extra time to make sure both nipples were completely clear of any traces of the smooth, sweet substance. For her efforts, she received a hungry growl and a spoonful of pudding on her neck.

He set the spoon back in the bowl and the bowl on the table, then gripped her hair in his fist and tugged slightly until she tipped her head to the side.

The first swipe of his tongue sent a blanket of goosebumps down one side of her body and the second one sent a wave of shivers. The third one made her knees weak and the fourth one made her dizzy. By the time he'd taken his first nip, she was as spineless and pliable as the substance he'd smeared on her.

The client book could wait a little while.

She pulled off her shirt and he unfastened her bra. She unzipped her jeans and he helped her out of them, shoving them down over her hips. His fingers stroked her wet sex through her satin panties and she moaned and dropped her head back.

Jake kneeled before her, kissing her thighs, her knees, her shins, her ankles as they were exposed by her descending pants. Then he pulled them off as she lifted first one foot and then the other, tossed her pants aside and nuzzled her pelvis. He audibly inhaled. "I love the way you smell."

Her breath hitched as he gently bit her labia. "I suppose that's better than being grossed out."

"There isn't a thing about you that grosses me out." He caught the waist of her panties with his thumbs and tugged them down over her hips. "You're the most beautiful, intelligent, sexy woman I've ever known."

"That's mighty kind of you to say. But you're only saying it because you want to get laid," she half-joked.

"No way." His fingers dug into her hips and he looked up into her eyes. "Look at me."

She dropped her gaze.

"I'm telling you right now that I adore you. You are the most precious, wonderful woman in the world. And even if you told me we couldn't make love again until our time was up I'd still say the same thing. Over and over and over again. Until you believed me."

Her cheeks warmed and she couldn't respond for a couple of stuttering heartbeats. What he'd said. How sincerely he'd said it. She couldn't possibly say the same to him. Yes, she liked him, more than she probably cared to admit. But after what he'd said, her confession would sound lame. Didn't even want to go there. It might hurt his feelings. Then again, saying nothing was probably no better.

Maybe distracting him was the best option? Redirection. "Why . . . thank you," she said. "But I'd be an idiot to tell you we couldn't make love." She lobbed her head from side to side. "Say, since I'm feeling rather stressed at the moment, how about you distract me for a while?"

As she expected, he said, "It would be my pleasure." He scooped her up with ease and tossed her over his shoulder like a caveman, then carted her back to the bedroom and lowered her onto the bed. The panties came off in a heartbeat and before she could blink an eye, he was kissing her between her legs and bringing her to a quick, soul-cleansing orgasm.

Then, as she fought to catch her breath, he removed his pants and pulled her toward him until her bottom was positioned at the very edge of the bed. Standing, he pushed himself into her, filling her completely. They groaned in unison, then he drew out and plunged deep again. Over and over. And when he pushed her knees back, the sensation intensified until she was hot and trembling and begging for release. When he traced slow circles over her sensitive nub she found that release. His pace quickened with the first spasm of her orgasm and she cried out in ecstasy as he poured his seed into her.

Then, flushed and gasping and sweaty, he flopped over top of her and gathered her into his arms. He pressed a kiss to her chin. "Thanks," he huffed.

"No, thank you." She tightened her inner muscles around his softening member. "That was wonderful." She wrapped her arms around his bulk and just lay there, relishing the scent of his skin and salty taste, the weight of him on top of her, and the fading tingles between her legs.

"That was magic, you know?" he said between heavy gasps. He pulled out of her and rolled to his side, taking her with him. Their legs hung over the side of the bed.

"Really? Can't say anyone's ever said that before."

"No, I mean the stuff I deposited. It's magic. Now you'll go back in there and find exactly what you were looking for."

She laughed. "Men! You guys are too funny. Like a bunch of swimmy-tailed bitty cells are going to solve all the woes of the world."

"Well, I didn't say that, exactly." When she gave him a "yeah right" look, he amended, "Okay, maybe I did. What I meant to say was that I have faith that the extra blood flowing to that adorable brain of yours is going to help you think better."

"I'll have to test your theory. And if you're right, well then, I can see us making a lot of love the next few days. It's always a good thing to have lots of blood flowing to the brain. Course, I always assumed blood was flowing to other places during sex, not the brain. But you're the doctor."

"That's right. So you can take my word for it." He kissed her softly, then pushed himself upright. A warm trickle ran down her leg as she stood. She went to the bathroom and cleaned up, then redressed and settled back at the kitchen table. She ate the rest of the pudding as she read through the *N*'s, nibbled on a few cookies as she skimmed the *O*'s and *P*'s, and enjoyed some chocolate candies as she read through the *Q*'s, *R*'s *S*'s and *T*'s.

Nothing stood out. Nothing! She felt the burning tears of frustration as she read through the *U*'s, *V*'s and *W*'s. When she found her name, however, her eyes came to a halt at an unfamiliar sequence of letters and numbers. It wasn't her address, phone number, or any other vital statistic she could think of.

Excited, she said, "I think I've found something."

"See? My blood-flow theory stands. What'd you find?" Jake asked, at her side in a split second. He dropped a kiss on her shoulder and leaned over it to read. "435Woodward 1984?"

"I didn't live on Woodward."

"That's a long street. Goes all the way from Detroit up to Pontiac."

"Do you think it's an address? What does the last part mean? A year, maybe?"

"Could be. Should we drive up and down Woodward and see what's at that address?"

"I don't think that makes sense. First, we don't have a car. Second, there are probably more than one 435 Woodward, considering how the addresses run north and south of the city changes. Woodward must go through a half-dozen cities, at least."

"Is that so? I haven't been down the full length of Woodward before."

"I did once when I got lost in downtown Detroit. Road construction. I hate it. And there should be a law against closing an entire freeway in the middle of the city during the summer."

He nodded with understanding.

"You wouldn't believe how scared I was."

"I bet. I'm glad to see you survived." He kissed the back of her neck. "But how're you going to find out what or who is located at 435 Woodward if you don't take a drive?"

"Maybe I can find something online." She shuffled to the computer and sat. "We can try Mapquest first." 435 Woodward, Detroit was right downtown by the river. She tried several more cities and found one more listing. "Well, there are only two that I can find. The Detroit listing, then one in Rochester."

"Now what?"

"I don't know. They're so far away from one another. There's no chance we could walk. And with Detroit's cruddy public transportation system, we'd be on a nasty bus all day if we tried to go the bus route." She turned around when Jake didn't respond. He was standing at the kitchen table, the leather book in his hand, staring at the page.

"What if it isn't an address? I mean, that seems obvious, but if he was trying to hide something, why would he make it so simple?" she asked.

"You have a point. That's practically like drawing red circles and putting stars around it."

She chuckled. "Exactly."

"But if it isn't an address, what is it?" he asked.

"That's a good question. What else could it be?"

"I don't know. That's why I asked you."

She thought for a moment. "Could be a locker."

"Yeah?"

"Like at a skating rink?" she added.

"Sure. Or a storage unit. Some company called Woodward something. Woodward Storage?"

"Crap. This is hard." She punched a few keys in frustration, shutting down the Mapquest windows.

"I have faith in you. You'll figure it out."

"Then you have more faith than I do," she confessed.

"That's my job as sidekick, isn't it?" he teased, setting the book next to her right hand on the table. "I'm supposed to have unshakable faith in you and ask a bunch of questions until your brilliant mind solves the puzzle. Could it be a password?"

"Password to what?"

"Computer? E-mail? Log in to some site?"

"Yeah. But boy oh boy. How will we ever figure it out?" She felt hope dwindling. She stared at the computer screen for a while but didn't know what to look at next. Deciding to check out the storage unit angle, she found the local yellow pages in a drawer—hoping he wouldn't have chosen a storage unit on the other side of town—and looked in the business white pages under "Woodward." She didn't find a single entry.

Was that a good thing or a bad thing?

Now tired and cranky and frustrated, she shut off the computer and flopped onto the couch. Jake was watching a movie. He pulled her into an embrace and kissed away her foul mood. Then he cooked her a delicious dinner. "Maybe tonight while you're back at Matt's place you'll find something to help you determine what that code means," he suggested as they ate broiled chicken breasts and vegetables. He made no more comments about Matt, the code, or anything else related to her death that evening.

After they ate, he ran a hot bubble bath for her, scrubbed her back with a scratchy scrubby thing, then gave her a long, thorough massage.

Later, she drifted off with her head resting on his shoulder and his arms flopped possessively over her stomach.

Anxious to poke around for clues, she arrived at Matt's house an hour early. She concentrated on searching his home office, looking through files and drawers for anything that caught her eye. Then she turned on his laptop computer. The Windows XP welcome screen appeared and she tried several likely passwords. When they all failed she powered it down and gathered the cords, stuffed it in the case, and, deciding he wouldn't mind if she borrowed it for a day or two, set it by the front door.

As she was turning to head back to the bedroom, someone twisted the doorknob. She lunged behind the silk ficus tree in the corner and hoped it was Matt at the door. She'd never heard of anyone being released from the hospital at nearly midnight but she supposed it was possible. Or maybe he'd been released earlier in the day but hadn't come straight home. The likelihood of it being Matt increased. She considered stepping out from behind her camouflage but didn't get too far before the door swung open.

In stepped one man, then a second. Neither of them was Matt. And both of them looked familiar. Eerily familiar.

It was them. The men who'd shot her.

As if someone had thrown a switch, she started quaking all over. She stepped back toward the wall, away from the fake greenery, to keep from brushing against it as she waited for them to do whatever vile, despicable thing they were about to do.

"No one's here. Let's just get this over with," said the taller one. Murderer Number One.

"I just want to make sure the dump's empty." Murderer Number Two skulked farther inside, poking his head into the living room and sweeping a flashlight beam through the room. "You go get started unloading the van."

"Yeah, yeah. I always get the backbreaking job."

Poor baby. If I could put you out of your misery, I would.

"Just go do it. I'll be right there." Murderer Number Two headed toward the back of the house.

Not sure if she would be invisible to them like she had been with Matt, Claire didn't budge from her hiding spot. Luckily, it was a deep corner. Very dark. Murderer Number Two's flashlight beam missed her twice as he continued his search.

It was too bad. The opportunity of a lifetime was right there in her face but she was afraid to take it. If she knew for a fact she couldn't be seen, she wouldn't hesitate to scare the crap out of these scumbags. Land them in a padded room for a while. But the prospect of getting shot again stopped her from even considering it.

Murderer Number One came inside carrying a big cardboard box. Something rattled inside. Glass. Metal. Why would crooks break into someone's house and bring stuff inside rather than take things out?

He walked back toward the kitchen. She heard him talking to Murderer Number Two, then the squeak of a door opening.

Standing on legs that were getting weaker by the second, from fear and the desperate need to reenergize, she forced herself to stay put. For now she was safe. After they were gone, she'd reenergize, then check and see what they were up to.

She just hoped they wouldn't be there too long.

They both walked back out the front door, then returned a minute later with more large boxes. They carted them toward the back of the house and didn't return for a while.

Her head was swimming now, the world tipping and tilting every time she moved it even a fraction of an inch. And her knees felt like they were made out of Jell-O. Her arms hung limply at her sides and her back was slumped. She couldn't hold it straight. She even felt her head lolling to one side.

She needed to get into that bedroom. Pronto!

She sank to the floor and leaned her spine against the wall.

"That oughta take care of him," one of them said. The other merely grunted. They walked past her out the front door and shut it.

She didn't wait to see if they were returning before she started crawling toward the bedroom. Her limbs felt stiff and heavy, like they were made of concrete, and her slow, labored breathing echoed in her head.

I'm not going to make it.

Thoughts of Jake, memories of sweet moments she'd shared with him the past few days, filled her mind as she dragged herself down the hallway. They kept her going, pushing her to struggle when she would rather have stopped. And, when she was sure she'd taken her last breath, she looked up. Matt's bed was right there. Just one more burst of energy. Just one more . . . just one more. . . .

She didn't have it in her.

I'm sorry, Jake. I'll see you in ten years. Hot tears slid down her cheeks. She let her eyelids fall closed and rested on the carpet. Her senses dulled until she couldn't feel what was under her or hear the faint tick tock of the wall clock anymore.

Then an obnoxious blaring sound startled her. What was that? It sounded like an alarm. It had to be loud for her to hear it at this point, so close to going.

Hoping the momentary rest had helped her gather a tiny bit of strength, she opened her eyes but they did little to help her. She was practically blind, could see nothing but black. She pushed herself up on all fours, then reached up and dragged her torso upright by pulling on what she hoped was the bedding. Almost there! Now determined, she gathered what strength she had and lunged up onto the bed and rolled onto her back. The red wet blob, which had probably been hovering over the bed, immediately sank into her.

Oh . . .

She felt her heartbeat quicken, her blood rushing through arteries and veins that had become pliable again. Muscles fed by the blood became resilient and strong. Energy charged through her system. And her senses became acute again. The smell of burning paper stung her nose and she jumped from the bed. A thick, dark cloud of smoke hung high up by the hallway ceiling. She now recognized the sound that had woken her as the whiny scream of a smoke detector.

Stooping low to avoid breathing too much of the smoke, she hurried toward the kitchen, where she knew the men had been. But right away, she noticed that the smoke wasn't coming from there. It was rolling up from the basement staircase.

Hearing the distant drone of fire trucks, she ran down the basement stairs to see what was going on.

Immediately, she noticed the metal trash can spewing noxious black smoke. That was the only source of it. There was no fire elsewhere, and, as she got closer, it became evident the men had intended it that way.

On a circa 1950s metal-framed kitchen table sat an array of little baggies full of white powder, scales, trays, bundles of cash, and several guns.

What the heck? She knew for a fact that Matt was not a drug dealer. He was being framed? Why? Worried because she knew time was short and she had to act quickly, she spun around.

Which first? Put out the fire or get rid of the condemning evidence? The fire looked like it was going out on its own. The eyeball-incinerating smoke had thinned out, so she focused her attention on the drugs.

The boxes the two stooges had carried the crap in were tossed in the corner. She grabbed one and hurried to throw the stuff inside. The roar of fire truck sirens growing louder by the second, she ran for a second empty box and basically swooped her arm across the table, sending the drugs and trays and money flying into the box. She knew she couldn't get all the white dust off the table, so she flipped the table over, and as the firemen beat on the front door, she dragged the heavy boxes back into the corner, flipped the tops closed, and hid herself behind the furnace.

Several minutes later two firefighters stomped down the stairs in their heavy coats. She heard more upstairs.

"A garbage can," one said. He filled the can with water from the hose, then looked down into the can. He reached down and picked something up, inspecting it before dropping it again. "Looks like someone wanted us to come down here."

"Wonder why," the second one said as he swiveled his head to look around. "Weird."

I know why but I'm not telling. Something tiny with way too many legs skittered up her arm and she jerked to knock it off. Dust and smoke stung her nose, tickling a sneeze, and she had to pinch it closed to keep from revealing her whereabouts to the firemen.

"Don't see anything else down here. Better tell the captain."

The men walked back up. Moments later the basement was in full illumination and firemen and policemen were all over the place. To stay hidden, she had to lay prone on the cold, damp concrete. That wasn't pleasant. It stank like old sweaty socks and the chill seemed to seep through her skin and into her bones. But she didn't dare move. The worst drawback: thanks to her position she couldn't see a thing anymore.

She heard one policeman talking on a police radio while another chatted with the firemen. Finally, the one who'd been yakking on the radio said, "We don't have a search warrant. Gotta go. Fire's out. There's no evidence of a crime."

The basement cleared. The lights were doused. Whew! Close call.

Now, what did it all mean, she wondered as she scraped herself off Matt's yucky basement floor. The guy was a clean freak, but it seemed there was at least one corner he'd neglected. She brushed dust balls and dead insect remnants off her clothes and out of her hair, then tiptoed toward the stairs.

Why would the guys who'd murdered her return after all these years, plant drugs and money in Matt's home, and then try to get him arrested?

Once she was sure the array of public servants had vacated the house, she ran up the stairs, grabbed the laptop on her way out, and headed back to Jake.

Just like that, things had changed—for the worse! This wasn't any longer just a matter of satisfying her curiosity. It was looking more like Matt was a victim, not a criminal. That thought was reassuring but also worrisome. Someone was out to get Matt and even though he wasn't her fiancé any longer, she couldn't just stand by and watch him be framed for drug dealing.

It was time to really step up her efforts. She hoped Jake would understand.

Chapter 17

Jake listened with growing rage and frustration to Claire's story. Damn it! He couldn't tell her not to go back to Matt's place. She had to. But the thought of her alone, facing the two men who'd shot her, made him see red. He could not care less about what they were trying to do to Matt. Good guy or not, he wasn't Jake's problem. The woman sitting next to him, trembling, was his problem. His entire being ached to protect her yet he knew he was frickin' powerless to do just that.

Shit, shit, shit!

"I can go with you tomorrow night," he offered.

"No, you can't!" she nearly shrieked. "Then you won't be able to reenergize . . . and you'll be gone . . . and I'll be alone. Call me selfish. I want you to stick around to the end. I need you to stick around." She wrapped her arms around his neck and pressed her soft body against his. He could smell the stench of smoke in her hair, on her clothes. The scent only inflamed his anger.

"I won't stand by and let you be hurt."

"I wasn't. I'm fine." She pushed away from him and waved her arms to illustrate. "There's not a mark on me."

"But there could've been. What if that fire had spread while you were in the bedroom? Or what if they'd stuck around another five minutes and you weren't able to reenergize? Sounds like you wouldn't have made it if they had."

"If, if, if." She stroked his cheek and stared into his eyes but he wouldn't be soothed. "Jake, you're sweet for worrying about me, but I'm okay. It worked out okay."

"This time."

"Yeah."

"What if they come back?"

"Then I'll be ready for them. I know what they're up to now. But I wonder why. Of course, if I could figure that out, I'd know why they shot me." She glanced down at her hands. "I only wish I'd had enough strength to look at the truck they'd been driving. That might've helped. I took too long snooping and put off reenergizing. But I won't make that mistake again," she said before he had a chance to warn her not to do that tomorrow night. She slumped against him again. "Please. Don't get all testosteroney and start spouting orders and lectures. I just want you to hold me tonight. Okay?" she said into his chest. "Just hold me."

It might kill him to hold his tongue, but he decided it was for the best—for now. He was too pissed off. Who knew what he might say. Maybe tomorrow, after he'd had some time to cool off, he could talk to her with a more level head about the situation.

They walked to the bedroom and fell into bed, still fully dressed. And he inhaled the stink of smoke as he cradled her in his arms, stroking her smelly hair, soft as satin. Her shaking slowly eased and her breathing became slow and shallow as she slipped into sleep. He held her tightly, still shaken by having almost lost her. Only The Man Upstairs knew if he'd ever find her again if he lost her. The thought of spending eternity searching for her made him so sad he wanted to weep.

Somehow he had to protect her.

Up until this point, he'd let her do the investigating pretty much on her own. He hadn't poked his nose in too much, just encouraged her, played the stupid sidekick, because he'd wanted her to find the answers for herself. He knew she'd feel better about doing it for herself. Her independent streak wouldn't allow him to get too involved.

But now . . . now he had to take a little more active role in the investigation, even if it was just keeping track of what she was doing. Sure, it didn't change the fact that he wasn't a detective. But he couldn't let her stumble into another dangerous situation.

His assumption had been wrong. He had thought this was a closed case, a dead hostility between Matt and some sick son-of-a-bitch woman-killer. Clearly the son-of-a-bitch woman-killer wasn't done with Matt yet. And he could guess a hostility that lasted more than nine years wasn't going to disappear without some major fireworks.

His job was simple: to keep Claire out of the middle of that. Somehow.

He pressed a kiss to her forehead and she stirred, smiling softly. Damn, she was beautiful.

Not solving this mystery sure beat the heck out of losing for an eternity the woman he loved. He hoped she would come to see things his way, even if it meant telling her everything.

"I'm going back to Matt's place this afternoon," Claire announced the next morning before she'd even gotten out of bed.

Jake groaned in response and hugged her tightly. "No, you're not."

Did he just tell me no? "Huh?" Caught off-guard and hoping she'd misunderstood, she asked, "What did you just say?"

"I said no, you're not going to Matt's house, not if I have any say in the matter."

"Well, you don't and yes, I am."

"I'm not going to let you go." His grip around her waist tightened and she wriggled to get free. Something was wrong here. This wasn't the Jake she'd spent the past few days with. Where'd he go? And who was this possessive stranger who'd taken his place? She studied his face for a moment, noting the flat expression. "Okay, okay. Joke's over. I'm not laughing. Now let me up."

"I'm not joking," he said flatly, still refusing to let her go.

"You can't hold me like this forever." Feeling like she was being held by a huge polar bear, she squirmed harder but his grip on her didn't slacken. Not a bit. Worn out and frustrated, she lay still for a moment. Obviously she was going to have to think herself out of this situation, not muscle herself out. Jake was way too strong for that. "Sooner or later you'll have to go to the loo."

"I'll take you with me."

"Gross!" She tipped her head up to look at his face. "Come on, what's with the caveman act today? I'm a grown woman. I can do what the heck I want."

"Just call me Grunt."

"Grrr!" She went back to wiggling, even started swinging her feet. If it took a solid kick in the balls to convince him he needed to let her go, so be it. No man told her what to do. Darn it, had she misread another man? Was Jake more controlling than she'd first thought? "Let go. I want to look at you when you answer my question."

"What question?" he mumbled, still not releasing her.

"This one. I want to make sure I've got this straight. You are telling me I'm not going to Matt's house at all today? Because if that's what you're saying, some fur's gonna fly."

"Yes. But I'm telling you that for your own good."

"Hello. I'm not a kid. I can take care of myself. And I've had enough of the caveman act. Let me the hell go!"

She wriggled and shoved and when that still didn't work, a quick motion of the knee toward his vitals brought her the desired results. She didn't even have to make contact. Smart man. Stupid for trying to boss her around, but smart enough to know real danger when he was staring it straight in the patella. She sat up, ran her hands through her hair, and glared down at Jake, the man who suddenly thought he owned her.

She should've known he was too good to be true. They always were.

On his side, he lifted himself on one arm. "Sorry. I'm not trying to be bossy. But I'm worried about you." He looked worried. He sounded worried. That cooled her temper slightly.

"Don't worry." She needed to pee. She stood.

"Easier said than done," he said with a soft chuckle.

"Well, do it anyway. We're both here for such a short time. I thought it was just to have fun, have sex, eat chocolate. But now I'm beginning to see it's for another reason, something deeper, more meaningful than even the one good deed we did Halloween day. That was nothing. But saving an old friend from—"

"Friend?" he interrupted, eyebrows up around the stratosphere. Ears the hue of cherries.

"Ahhh . . . I get it now. You're jealous of Matt. You don't like that I care."

"Do not . . . am not." Now his cheeks were as red as his ears. And his neck. The color was moving south. She wondered how far down she could make it go.

"Are too. Look at you. You look like you spent the last week frying in the sun, lobster boy." That little jab made the deep burgundy shade spread down across his chest.

"I care about you. Is that such a crime?" he blurted, sitting up and mussing his hair with his hands. "I'm not a jealous control freak. I just don't want you to get hurt. It kills me to think I almost lost you yesterday. . . ."

Kills him?

"That you might've been killed again and I wouldn't know how to find you. . . ."

Find me.

"That I had finally gotten you . . ."

Huh? Gotten me?

". . . only to lose you so soon." His bottom lip trembled as he looked her in the eye. Still, his expression wasn't soft or weak. It was intense and frightening and adorable. "I'll spend the rest of eternity looking for you if I have to. I'm not going to lose you again."

"Oh." That's all she could say.

"I have a confession to make," he said.

"You mean that last bit wasn't a confession?"

"It was. But I have more to confess."

"Okay. Should I sit down?"

"Maybe." He patted the mattress, then waited for her to sit before he continued. "Claire, before we both died I was watching you. I noticed you years ago, before you were engaged to Matt. I wanted to ask you out."

Wow! I didn't see that coming. Feeling blindsided, she asked, "Why didn't you ask me out?"

"I was a struggling resident at the time. No money. Crazy hours."

"Oh."

"Then I finished up my residency and joined my partner in his practice and things settled down. But by then you and Matt were involved and I didn't feel right trying to come between you. I figured you were happy."

She didn't respond to that last part, mainly because spending the last few days with Jake had made her see what real happiness was. And it wasn't what she'd had with Matt.

"I watched and waited, hoping you might break up with him, but you didn't. You got engaged instead. Then, I decided life was too short and I had to tell you how I felt. But I died the day before I was going to tell you."

"Oh." She could tell by the way he was looking at her he wanted her to say something, more than monosyllabic grunts. But she had to admit she was speechless. It was all still sinking in, the notion of him pining from afar, waiting for her to be available, hoping he might someday have a chance with her. And her being so blind to it all that time. It all was so sad . . . sad but sweet.

"I've waited almost fifteen years to hold you, to hear you utter my name in passion, to make love to you."

"Then it was no accident we bumped into each other at Devil's Night."

"I was hoping you'd be there. I didn't know you'd passed. I just wanted to tell you how I felt. To finally have it off my chest." He set his hand on top of hers.

She glanced down at his hand, then up at his face again. She searched it for the truth. "But you waited this long after we'd found each other, instead of telling me right away. Why?"

"Well, yeah," he admitted, looking sheepish and guilty. "You said you wanted no-strings sex and that made me doubt the wisdom in admitting my feelings, since I couldn't give you more than a week and a half of physical bliss. So I kept my mouth shut."

"But you knew I was also a Spirit American, at least by the next day."

"Yeah. Later. You've been a little preoccupied. I was just waiting for the right moment to tell you."

"I have been preoccupied. Sorry. This mystery thing has kind of taken me over." Now she felt guilty. Here they had the opportunity to spend just a precious few days together and she was insisting those precious moments be spent chasing around a couple of lowlife scumbags . . . who were trying to frame an old friend of hers . . . and who deserved to spend the rest of their natural lives in jail.

"I understand why this means so much." He ran a hand up and down her back. Such an innocent touch, yet it sparked a fire between her legs. "But I can't sit idly by and watch you put yourself in danger."

"I understand." She had never felt as cherished as she did right then, as he caressed her back and looked at her with such concern and . . . and love? Her heart swelled. "But I feel bad for Matt. I don't love him anymore but I can't sit here and not do something. He should at least know what's going on."

"Then why don't you go to the hospital and tell him? Let him handle it with the authorities."

She nodded. "That sounds like a reasonable suggestion. I thought about going there before but figured they might not let me see him."

"They may not, but it's worth a try. Right?"

"Yeah. Okay. Will you come with me?"

"I'll go to the hospital. But I won't go into the room with you. That would be kind of . . . uncomfortable . . . considering . . ."

"Fair enough."

"Let's get a shower, have some breakfast, then we'll head to the hospital." He gathered her into a warm, rumpled, sleepy man embrace. He smelled wonderful, of cotton sheets and man. He felt incredible, powerful, tight muscles encased in satiny skin. His steady thudding heartbeat soothed her.

Moments later, she forced herself to break free of his grasp and head into the shower. She made quick work of getting ready and while he cleaned up, she scarfed down some cereal. She waited impatiently—she really did need to do something about her lack of patience, someday—as he ate. About an hour after they'd risen they were out the front door and on their way to the hospital.

* * *

Riverside was a small hospital. A relatively new construction, made out of brick and looking more like an office building than a hospital, it wasn't but a couple of miles from their apartment. Which meant she didn't have long to plan her speech to the nurse or whoever regulated the visitors coming and going to the psychiatric ward.

Miracle of all miracles, they walked in, followed the sign to the psychiatric ward, rode the elevator to the second floor, and passed an empty nurses' station. It was so easy it made her worry.

Jake waited by the elevators as she wandered up and down the hallway, looking for Matt's name on the little paper labels next to the doors.

Down at the very end she found his name, knocked, then entered.

Matt was lying on the bed, snoring loudly. He looked very tired. Dark circles hung under his eyes. Deep lines etched into his rough skin on his forehead and around his mouth, making him appear much older than his thirty-something years. She hated waking him. After a moment's hesitation she poked his shoulder and he stirred.

"Matt?" she whispered. "It's Claire. I need to talk to you. I hope you can see me now."

"Huh?" His eyes were still closed.

"Can you hear me?"

"Yeah," he grumbled. "Cla-a-a-a-aire?" he asked, sounding stoned. She wondered if he knew where he was.

"Yes, it's Claire. Are you okay?"

"Yea-a-a-ah . . ." His eyes still closed, he smiled like a druggie who'd just shot up. "Yea-a-a-a-ahhh . . . go-o-o-o-o-od . . ."

"Listen closely. Okay? I need to tell you something. A couple of men broke into your house. They put some illegal drugs in your basement and then lit a fire so the police and fire would come and discover them. Do you know who would do this?"

"Yea-a-a-ah."

"Who, Matt? Who would do this?" She leaned in closer so she could hear but immediately wanted to lunge backward. Ick. Matt needed a sponge bath. She wrinkled her nose and tried not to inhale through it. "Who would want to see you put in prison?"

"Mrrggghhh."

"Who?"

"Bas-s-s-stard."

"Bastard. Yeah. He's a bastard. Who is it? I want to help you. I want to stop him."

He blinked open his eyes. They shifted to the right, then left.

"Can you see me?" she asked.

"Claire?"

"Yep, it's me."

He sat bolt upright and screamed, flailing his arms around her, ripping at IV tubes and his hospital-issue gown. One hand reached down under the covers and then resurfaced with what she guessed might be a catheter.

She tried to shush him but he wouldn't be shushed. His voice a shrill wail, it brought in a pair of nurses and several bulky men. They rushed past her, pushed him back on the bed, and secured his arms and legs in straps. The covers were tossed back, exposing Matt's tender parts as a nurse went about reinserting the catheter he'd not-so-gently ripped out while another one searched his arm for a vein to reinsert his IV.

"It's okay, Mr. Gerald. You just relax and we'll have you feeling better in no time," one nurse softly crooned as she ripped open plastic packages holding various medical supplies.

"That's strange. He was doing so much better. He was

going to be released today," said the second nurse as she too rummaged through drawers and gathered supplies.

"Guess we'd better tell the doctor. He might want to change his medication," said the first nurse as she held his penis in her fist and threaded a new catheter into it.

Claire cringed. It looked extremely painful.

Feeling out of place, she crept out quietly. She answered Jake's questioning gaze with, "He's so doped up I doubt he'll remember a thing I told him." She sighed and sagged against him as he stood and wrapped an arm around her shoulders.

"Sorry, babe."

"Which means he's still a target. He doesn't have a clue what's going on. I never would've believed it if I hadn't seen it with my own eyes. He went berserk. Ripped out his IV and Foley. Screamed like a little girl."

"Chances are he wouldn't go to jail, even if those bastards are able to plant drugs in his place."

"You never know. I asked him who would do such a thing."

"And?" he asked as he gently led her into the elevator.

"He said 'Mfffrghhhh', whatever that means. Or maybe it was 'Mrrrggghh'. Yeah, I think that was it."

"Okay. Well, sounds like it might start with an *M*. So that's something. Let's go back and see if we can piece together some things."

"So you aren't going to make me to give this up?"

He smiled, his eyes twinkling. "I couldn't."

"Thank you for understanding, Grunt."

The doors opened on the main floor just in time for a lobby full of people to see her throw her arms around his neck and shove her tongue into his mouth.

Chapter 18

"I'm anxious to hear. What do you think 'Mrrrgggghhh' means?" Back at the apartment, reclining on the couch, staring at the midsection of Jake as he stood before her, Claire made herself comfy, figuring they'd be there a while.

"Could be a lot of things. Most likely someone's name."

"Ick," she joked. "I wouldn't want to go by a name like that. Imagine growing up with a name like Mrrrgggghhh? Oh, the teasing that poor schmuck must've endured. No wonder he's a criminal."

He chuckled. She watched, realizing just how much she adored that sound and loved the way his eyes glittered. Little happy crinkles formed at the corners.

"Let's see what we can find." She swept up the book of customers in her hand and flipped it open to *M*'s. There were lots of them. Too many. "Ugh. There are more than twenty names here. None of them look anything like Mrrrgggghhh."

"Any of them have an address on Woodward?" Jake asked, sitting next to her. His arm rubbed slightly against hers. It was a pleasant friction that made her momentarily hungry for another kind of friction. He leaned closer, reading, "What about names with an *R* in them?"

"Still too many," she answered, skimming the addresses.

"This is very frustrating." She sighed and lifted her eyes to his face. The sight of his whiskered chin and yummy lips, oh-so-close, made her sigh again. Maybe she needed another distraction. "So, did you mean what you said earlier? Are you going to help me now?"

"I wanted to let you do it yourself, but now it's too dangerous. I'll do what I can to help."

"Thanks. I'm not too proud to admit I'm in over my head."

He nudged her shoulder. "Another reason to love you."

There it was again. The *L* word. But this time it didn't stir such discomfort. She didn't feel like running away. No, not at all. Instead her palms got damp and her heart grew three sizes, like in the Grinch movie. Her eyes burned. She was an emotional train wreck in the making. If he said it again, she was likely to fall into his arms, blubbering like a soap star.

"Are you all right?" He stared into her eyes, which, she imagined, were in need of some Visine.

She blinked a few times. "Yeah. It's just the stress, I suppose. And I wonder . . ." She couldn't finish the sentence. Even the thought of going back to purgatory and not seeing him for ten whole years made her ache all over.

He gently gripped her shoulders and pulled until she turned her upper body to face him square on. "What, baby?"

"I just wonder . . . if we'll be able to find each other after we go back."

"I wonder too. If we can't, promise me the next time you reanimate you'll come back to Devil's Night." His eyes were pleading as they delved into hers. "Please."

She nodded. "In front of Devil's Night. But I don't want to wait ten years."

"Oh, baby." He drew her to him and wrapped his thick arms around her. "Neither do I. I waited this long and now that I have you, I don't want to let go for anything. You're mine, damn it."

That possessive tone didn't bother her like it might've in the past either. In fact, she was overjoyed by it. She started running her hand up and down his back in a gentle caress. The thump of his heartbeat in her ear, the scent of his skin tickling her nose, and the way he clung to her stirred latent lust. Need sparked and burned, singeing her veins as it spread. "Jake?" she whispered, tipping her head. She ached to feel his lips pressed to hers, to taste him, and feel his hard angles against her softer body. To feel sweat-slicked skin slide over hers.

"Yes, baby." He bent his head and angled his lips over hers.

She opened her mouth to sigh and he slipped his sweet tongue inside. It plunged and writhed. Hot hunger pooled in her belly. She stroked his tongue with hers and reached under his shirt to touch his belly. Soft over hard. Soft hair and satiny skin over rigid muscles. She felt them ripple and clench under her fingertips and moaned into his mouth. She swore she felt his skin flame, and she slipped her other hand under his shirt to see.

He broke the kiss and pulled off her shirt. She helped him out of his too—one good turn deserved another. He pulled the shoulder straps of her bra down over her shoulders until they hung over her upper arms, then pushed one lace demi-cup down, exposing her breast. Before he even touched it, her nipple hardened, poking out and begging for his warm mouth.

He kindly obliged, but not before rasping his velvet tongue over it first and gently scraping his teeth against the pink tip.

Her back tightened and arched, pushing her chest forward. Her breathing quickened and a warm pool of liquid need settled between her legs. What this man did to her!

He closed his warm, moist mouth over her nipple and suckled, drawing on it in a steady, erotic rhythm and her stomach muscles began to clench and release in time with it. Her head was spinning, so she closed her eyes and let it fall back. She felt his fingers in her hair as he caught it in one of his hands, hands that did magical, wondrous things to her body.

He pulled gently on her hair and she dropped her head back farther. Then he ran his tongue up the column of her neck in one long, damp, tingly line. When he nibbled, she shivered, hot and cold at the same time.

Her empty canal tightened around itself and she shuddered. "Jake," she murmured.

"Yes, baby," he answered against her neck. His lips tickled her sensitive skin, sending more goosebumps down her arms.

"I need you," she confessed.

"I need you too." He brought her hand to the lump in the front of his pants to illustrate.

"No, I need you," she corrected, knowing she was in no state to communicate clearly at the moment but compelled to try anyway. "I need you like I've never needed anybody."

In answer, he stood and swept her into his arms. She wrapped her arms around his thick neck as he carried her to the bedroom and lowered her onto the bed. Their gazes locked.

"Claire, if there is anything I can do to help it, we'll be together forever." He caught her chin in his hand and ran a thumb over her lips. "I promise."

She nodded and drew his thumb into her mouth. Her tongue swirled around the tip, licking it like a sweet lollipop, then she sucked, drawing it deeper inside.

He watched her with fire in his eyes, then pulled his hand away to undress her. He pressed on her chest, easing her onto her back, then unsnapped her jeans. He kissed and nipped her stomach, which sent needles of desire down to the apex of her thighs. She clamped her legs closed and squeezed against the burn. Naturally, it didn't help.

Taking advantage of her position, Jake slid her jeans down over her hips and legs. When they cleared her feet, he sent them sailing across the room. They landed with a soft *whoosh* on the floor.

He captured her hips in his hands and lifted them, rubbing his stubble-coated jaw over her satin-covered mound. The delicious friction left her moaning in sweet agony.

He let his hands slide lower until his fingers were burning the skin of her thighs. He gently urged them apart, then lowered his hot mouth over the apex of her thighs. Even through her panties the intimate touch sent waves of pulsing heat through her body. Parts all over trembled and tensed.

"You taste sweeter than anything," he murmured. "And I love the way you smell." He audibly inhaled. "I want to smell you forever."

He reached down and dug her fingers into the hard thick flesh of his shoulders. He groaned, then caught her panties in his fingertips and ripped them away. He parted her swollen, sensitized nether lips apart and slid his tongue down her slit. Now in utter bliss, her whole body aching for release, she ground herself into his face. His nose brushed against her nub and she cried out. When his tongue dipped in to taste her deeper, her thighs parted wider and trembled.

"That's it, baby. Give in to me. Give me everything."

She wanted release more than she wanted her next breath yet it still eluded her. Seeming to know how close she was, he pressed two fingers into her slit and stroked his hot tongue over the center of her pleasure until the world closed in on itself, leaving only her body and his, tumbling through space.

A powerful orgasm overtook her like a tsunami. She shuddered and moaned, trembled and tingled. Her inner muscles pulsed around his fingers for several aching moments.

He pulled them out and she opened her eyes, catching the fiery hunger in his eyes. Instantly, her lust reignited. He unfastened his jeans and disposed of them quickly, then rid himself of his snug cotton boxers too. His thick erection thrust forward, at ready, and she trembled at the thought of it sliding deep into her.

He climbed up on the bed. On hands and knees, he crawled over top of her. She could smell herself on his face as he leaned down to kiss her. And could taste herself on his tongue. Sweet and musky.

His erection poked her stomach; then, as he adjusted his position and settled his hips between her thighs, it pushed insistently at her perineum. He rocked his hips back and forth, back and forth and his rod rubbed against her slit, making her insides ache to be filled. She quivered with anticipation when the tip found her opening.

With slow torture it inched inside. The pleasure was profound, better than anything in heaven or on Earth. She lifted her legs and spread them wider, knowing it would intensify the sensation.

It worked and she groaned in satisfaction and licked his neck. Salty. It tasted salty and like Jake. His scent filled her nostrils. His weight pressed down on her. His hands lifted her head and cradled it gently. He kissed her closed eyelids as he slowly drew out, then thrust back in.

This wasn't the kinkiest sex she'd had in her life. The position was traditional. She wasn't tied up or being spanked. But it was the most wonderful sex of her life. Mind, body and soul, he touched them all. He murmured sweet words in her ears, promises of everlasting love as he drove into her. Her heart both swelled and hammered at her breastbone, threatening to explode as her mind tried to sort out the promises he uttered and the tastes on her tongue and the scents in the air and the touches he lavished on her body. Although she wanted release, she also dreaded it, knowing it would mean the magic would end. In this place, at this moment, they were the only souls that existed. The beauty of all creation was in his touch, his sigh, his scent.

When he quickened his pace, she knew she could hold back no longer. Orgasm claimed her in its relentless grip, carrying her to a faraway place where only pulsing heat and wild abandon existed. It was a fleeting visit. As he slowed, she returned to him and relished his final thrusts as he spilled his seed into her.

When he was spent, he sagged against her, not quite resting all his weight on top of her. His heavy breathing sawed in and out of his lungs, puffing against her neck. His slick chest slid against hers and, as he shifted, made funny noises against her breasts.

She giggled.

"What's so funny?" he said to her shoulder. He bit it.

"If sex wasn't so . . . wow . . . it might actually be funny."

"Funny?"

Hearing bruised ego in his voice, she amended, "Forget the funny. It was just wow. Wow, wow, wow. And did I say wow?"

He chuckled, pulled his flaccid member from her, rolled his not-so-flaccid body off her, and smiled into her eyes. "That good, eh?"

The ego was repaired. She snuggled up to him, resting her head on his chest and flopping an arm over his stomach. "Better than good. The best."

"Good."

"No, the best."

"Got it. So . . ." He ran his hand down her back and patted her bottom. "Wanna see if I can top that last one on the wow scale?"

"You betcha."

He hugged her to his chest and rolled her onto his stomach, and with wicked, wicked eyes, made her melt.

"Promise me you won't do anything crazy," Jake demanded, barring the door with his sexy, solid, yummy bulk.

She rolled her eyes in fake insult. "Moi? Crazy? Never."

"You're not making me feel any better about this."

"Well, unfortunately for you, you can't stop me. I have to go to Matt's."

"Grrr!" He lunged forward and caught her in his arms. She gladly sunk into his embrace, a part of her nervous about returning to Matt's house after what had happened the night before. Chances were nothing would happen—unless the bad guys had discovered their little ploy had failed. Jake tickled her unmercifully as she twitched and jerked, trying to block his hands from finding her most ticklish spots.

With no choice but to relent—or pee her pants—she said, "Okay, okay! I promise I won't do anything crazy like take on the bad guys by myself . . . unless they start it." He gave her bottom a swift smack and she yelped in surprise. "All right. I promise if they come back I'll hide until they're gone, just like I did before."

"Good." He glanced at his watch. "I'll be waiting for you in bed. Naked."

"Now that's the kind of scene any girl would be eager to come home to. I'll get back as fast as I can." She kissed him, then ran out the door, glad she'd left plenty early so she wouldn't be dragging herself into the bedroom, literally on her last breath. Fearful the two murderers had returned, she was careful to be very quiet and checked each room. She reenergized quickly, then headed straight to the front door.

A rattle at the knob sent her right back to her hiding spot behind the ficus tree. Darn it! These guys weren't going to give up!

They entered emptyhanded and silent, walked straight back toward the basement, obviously looking for the stuff they'd left last night. Despite Jake's warning playing like a skipping record through her head, she followed them on tiptoes, ducking behind pieces of furniture or walls as she went. She didn't go down to the basement but instead stood up at the top of the stairs, listening.

"What the hell? Who could've moved it? Shithead's in the damn hospital."

"Maybe he has someone watching his house."

"Shit. We'd better get outta here. Wherever the shit is, it can't be traced to us."

That declaration gave Claire an idea. Her mind sprang to life, working over the idea. What if she could somehow turn the tables and plant that crap on them? That would be sweet revenge—no, justice. She had to find a way.

They didn't see her as they hurried through the kitchen. She followed them, this time determined to get a look at whatever vehicle they were driving. She hoped she'd be able to look up their license plate on the Internet or something, somehow find out where they lived. She tiptoed behind them, so anxious to get to the front door before they sped off, she wasn't as careful as she should've been. She ran smack-dab into a lamp. It fell over.

The two murderers spun around. "Who's there?" one of them said.

Sure they'd seen her when the flashlight glared in her eyes, she lifted the fallen lamp to use as a weapon.

As she watched, all color drained from the men's faces. It was comical, and if she hadn't been ready to pee her pants from fear, she would've laughed until she peed.

"Wha-a-a-at the hell?" one of them screeched.

"I . . . uh . . . oh . . ." stuttered the other.

Wow. She felt so empowered. Who would've thought two murderers would be scared of a woman with a floor lamp? It wasn't even all that heavy. She stepped forward, testing their reaction.

Their eyes wide with terror, they skittered backward.

She lunged forward, thrusting the lamp at their midsections.

One of them squealed like a poked pig. To her surprise, they didn't reach for the guns safely tucked in harnesses on their chests.

"What's wrong, fellas? Afraid of poorly made decorating accessories?"

"Did I just hear a woman's voice?" said the short one.

"I . . . don't . . . know . . ." stuttered the big one.

They couldn't see her, but they could hear her? Oh boy, this was going to be fun!

"You couldn't possibly be afraid of a dead woman, now, could you?" She waved the lamp.

"Huh?" they said in unison.

"Did you hear something?" Shortie asked.

"What'd you think? You could shoot a woman in cold blood in her own bed and not pay for it?" she shouted, now jerking the lamp back and forth.

"Shi-i-i-it. That nut job was right. This place is haunted," shortie said.

"Oh, he's no nut job. He's my ex-fiancé. And he's only an ex because you figured you'd kill me," she growled in the most threatening voice she could muster. Watching grown men shake in their boots was so amusing it kind of took the edge off her anger. "Wanna tell me why you did it?" she asked, thrusting the lamp at their faces.

"Tell me I'm dreaming," Shortie said to the tall one, his teeth chattering as he spoke. "Frickin' pinch me or something. I gotta wake up from this nightmare."

"Here, I'll help." She shoved the lamp right at his gut, hard. The pointed finial at the top—at the moment she couldn't remember what it was called—poked at his belly.

The front of his pants slowly stained dark. Yippee! She'd made another grown man urinate in his pants.

"Do you usually wet yourself when you're sleeping?" she asked mockingly.

"Shit!" the other one said. Like a cockroach caught on a counter when the lights were flipped on, he scampered away, dashing for the door. He escaped before she could stop him, which left just Shortie.

Shortie watched his buddy do the I'm-gonna-save-my-ass-I'm-outta-here-routine with widening eyes, then tried to follow him out the door.

Naturally, Claire wasn't about to let him get away so easily. She had questions she wanted answers to. She lunged forward and, swinging the lamp, slammed the door a fraction of a second before it was too late.

Shortie jumped back and yelped, staring at the lamp. She could see him breathing hard, his chest rising and falling rapidly. Poor baby. He was scared poopless. Served him right!

She dropped the lamp and walked to the door, locking it. He watched the deadbolt as she turned it. "You're not going anywhere until I have some answers."

"I . . . don't . . . know anything, lady, or whoever you are. Don't hurt me."

"Sure you do. And you're gonna spill it or I'm going to make your life living hell from this point on. Contrary to popular belief, as a ghost I don't have to stay in this house. I can follow you everywhere. I can make things happen at any time. You want to spend the rest of your life scared, watching over your shoulder for someone you can't see?"

"Don't hurt me."

"Start talking."

He mumbled and cried like a little kid who'd had his ice

cream taken. Darn it! She couldn't understand a single word.

Someone knocked on the front door, interrupting her interrogation. Who the heck would be paying Matt a visit in the wee hours?

She peered through the peephole.

Jake. He wasn't naked. He wasn't in bed. And he wasn't looking particularly thrilled. Wait until he comes in.

She unlocked the door to let Jake in. But the minute the lock disengaged and the door opened, Shortie dashed past. Jake stood agape, watching the man run like a greyhound let out of the gate.

"Stop him!" she cried.

Jake spun on his heels and looked at the back of the retreating man, then shifted his gaze to her. His expression was fierce. No, seething would be a better word for it. Yeah, seething with a touch of incredulity. "What. Did. You. Do?"

"Nothing." She took several steps back.

"Nothing? I just watched a grown man run out of here like he'd seen a frickin' ghost."

"He did . . . er, kinda. He actually couldn't see me. Just like Matt."

"He couldn't?" Jake said, clearly surprised.

"Nope." She grinned. "I scared the patooties outta him. It was kind of fun. But just before I got some information from him you let him go."

"That's not my fault. I came here figuring you might be in trouble. How was I supposed to know you were playing interrogator with your murderer?"

She sighed. "Darn it. I was so close to getting the answers I wanted! I didn't even get their license plate."

"We'll find out who they were. Don't worry."

"I doubt they'll come back here now. Not after the scare I gave them."

He gathered her into his arms. "I'm sorry, baby. If I'd

known, I wouldn't have opened the door. I was worried about you."

"It's okay. Like you said, you didn't know." She pressed her ear to his chest and sunk into his warmth. "Let's go home. I'm tired."

"Now that's an idea I can go for. At least you won't have to worry about them coming back here to hurt Matt. I doubt they'll ever get near this place again."

"True. But that just means they'll try something else. And I might not be there to stop them."

Chapter 19

Bone tired after not sleeping a wink the next several nights, Claire dragged her heavy frame out of bed at almost noon. She skipped breakfast and went straight for lunch: a turkey sandwich, chips, and of course, dessert. The whole time she ate, she stared blindly at Matt's address book, flipping through the *M* pages, hoping she would catch something she'd missed earlier. Of course, the blurry, scratchy eyes didn't help. She blinked a lot and saw very little of what she was trying to read.

Finally, she slammed the book shut, shoved the dishes away, and dropped her face into her hands.

Strong hands came out of nowhere and kneaded her tense shoulders. "That bad?"

"I'm just tired."

"Why not forget it? You've been at this for days."

"Because I have only today left—just over twelve hours. And if I don't figure out who those guys are and what they want, an innocent man could be hurt. At least, I think he's innocent. I'm not completely sure about that yet either. I can't give this over to the cops since they wouldn't believe me if I told them the whole story. And I'm out of money, so I can't hire a private detective, not that I believe one of those guys would help me either."

"Maybe this is just the way it's supposed to be," he said behind her, his strong fingers working the kinks out of her neck.

She closed her eyes. "I can't believe that. I just can't. Like I said before, I think we came here for a reason, more than to have fun and sex and eat chocolate—as great as those things are. After all, The Big Guy's never been real keen on self-indulgence."

"You have a point." He drew up a chair next to her. "Have you figured anything else out?"

"No. Your suggestion to call all the people with names starting with *M* to see if they're still clients got me nowhere. Just lots of voice mailboxes."

"I was hoping . . ."

"Me too."

"What about at Matt's place? Did you do any more snooping over there?"

"Haven't found a thing. Believe me, if I had, you would've been the first to know. You couldn't help me much without all the facts. We're partners in this."

"I wasn't so sure about that. You haven't talked about it much the past couple of days. I was beginning to think you wanted to do this alone."

"No, I don't."

"What about the laptop? Did you get anything from it?"

"I can't figure out the password. I've tried every one I could think of, including the Woodward code we found next to my name." She smacked her flat palms on the table. The impact stung, but not more than the defeat burning up her insides. "Darn it! I was hoping I'd see those creeps pay for what they did. Isn't there any justice in this world?"

"What can I do?"

"I don't know. Nothing, I guess." She stretched her

arms over her head. "I think I need to just get up and move around a little. I'm stiff. Maybe I'll take a walk."

"Okay. I was going to head over to the store for a couple of things for dinner tonight. Would you rather I went with you?"

"No, that's fine. I could use the alone time, I think."

"Okay."

It was a crisp fall day, very chilly. The wind blew sharp gusts that stung her nose and ears, yet the sky was clear, the hue a brilliant blue. Lost in her thoughts, she walked with no real plan or destination in mind. Eventually she found herself in front of Matt's office, staring up at the old Victorian building, wishing a clue would fall into her lap but knowing that would be impossible.

Remembering the pretty garden behind the parking lot, the one part of the place that didn't give her the heebie-jeebies, she walked down the narrow driveway between his building and the next one, a similar house converted into a hair salon. As she walked across the parking lot toward the garden at the rear, voices coming from the back of the building made her glance over her shoulder.

The murderers! At Matt's office? And who were they talking to? They were both standing on the rear porch, their backs turned toward her, as they chattered with someone inside. Then a third man joined them, a man who was not quite as tall as the tallest one but taller than Shortie. He was thick, with a leather jacket . . . that looked damned familiar . . . Jake?

He followed the two men as they got into an unmarked white van. And as they sped by her, just barely missing plowing her over, he sat between them. For a split second, their gazes met, and even though they hadn't had more time than that, she'd read the guilt in his eyes.

What was he doing with the bad guys? Was he one of them?

Shoot! If he was, she was absolutely the worst judge of character in all history!

Confused, the niggling doubt that Jake was as great as he'd seemed all this time making her want to believe the worst, she hurried back to the apartment. She stomped around for a while in a rage, chastising herself for letting herself be so blind and stupid. She'd accepted everything he'd told her at face value. No one told the truth one-hundred percent of the time.

Dumb, dumb, dumb!

She needed to get busy doing something. She had nervous energy to burn, and pacing the floor, rehearsing her interrogation of Jake when he returned, would get her nowhere. Instead she went back to the computer and really thought about Matt and what was most important to him. What had been meaningful to him besides the obvious?

She thought about his home, thought about the conversations they'd shared during the time they dated.

Something came to mind. She typed "marge42," his mother's name and year of birth, into the Windows sign-in screen.

The computer charged to life, whirring and crackling as his desktop opened. She'd done it! Why hadn't she thought of that earlier?

Now, to find something, anything that would give her a hint to what was going on.

She skimmed the contents of his documents, used the search feature to look for the words *money*, *scam*, *con*, *fraud*. Nothing came up. She skimmed his letters and e-mails. She opened an Internet window and read through his favorites.

Yahoo! Groups was at the top of his list. That had to be significant. She'd never used Yahoo! Groups before. But she'd read they were a handy place to hide files one didn't want found. She hooked up the laptop to a phone line. Luckily his username and password for the Internet were stored in the memory. Within seconds she was online. She typed his name as a username for Yahoo! and on a whim tried the Woodward code. His groups opened. She found one in the short list with only one member, Matt.

She opened the group and, hoping he might have some hidden files stashed there, went to the files section. There, she found several Word documents.

Her hands shaking, sure she was on the verge of getting her answers, she opened the oldest one.

It was a diary of sorts. And it explained a lot, but not everything. She read every word, not quite absorbing the full meaning. His partner, Ben, was involved in money laundering? Sweet Ben with the even sweeter wife and house full of kids? Couldn't be!

She opened the second one. It was a letter Matt had written to the IRS, informing them of Ben's activities. She could see where this was going.

The third was another diary entry, detailing how Ben had threatened Matt, then how his goons had shot Claire to keep Matt from talking. Matt listed names, addresses, phone numbers. He included detailed descriptions of the lies he'd told the police and where he'd hidden the evidence.

Claire felt ill. Her stomach convulsed, sending its contents into her throat.

Ben, the man she'd sat with at dinner, laughed with, joked with . . . the man who she'd admired and trusted had hired someone to kill her, all in an effort to keep his skinny ass out of jail for hiding some jerk's illegal income!

How could she be so wrong about a person? Ben Murdock was a ruthless killer.

As if she hadn't been enraged before, now she was livid. Her heart was beating so hard and so fast it was leaving her breathless. And she trembled from head to toe. That was it. Ben would have to pay for what he'd done.

And if he hadn't moved recently, she knew where he lived.

She considered her options, and she had plenty. She could take the laptop, disable the passwords, and let the police learn the truth about her murder. But how would she get it to them? Just dropping it off at police headquarters wouldn't guarantee they'd look at the contents.

No, she had to make it look like evidence of a crime. . . .

The drugs . . .

Yeah, that would work.

Before she shut down the machine, she disabled the Windows password and then changed Matt's Yahoo! password and downloaded all the Word documents to his desktop for easy access. Now the police would read them all. His name would be cleared and Murdock, the murdering bastard, would pay the price for his crimes.

She shut down the computer and with it tucked safely under her arm, hurried back to Matt's place.

She checked to make sure he wasn't home from the hospital before letting herself in, then went downstairs to gather all the crap Murdock had hired his goons to plant in Matt's basement. Two huge boxes plus a metal trash can.

She borrowed a pair of winter gloves, just in case Spirit Americans left fingerprints, and loaded the whole lot into the trunk of Matt's car—thank goodness he had left it at the house. She found an extra set of keys in his desk drawer, threw the laptop in the passenger seat, then drove out of the driveway and to Ben's sprawling farmhouse a few miles west. She read "Murdock" on the mailbox stationed like a centurion at the intersection between the meandering driveway and the rutted dirt road.

There wasn't a car in sight as she followed the gravel drive up to the house. No cars, no kids, no people. She knocked and received no answer, and, hoping he was truly out of town, she tried the door to the breezeway. Locked. Evidently the criminal—Ben—wasn't as trusting as the innocent guy—Matt.

It was getting late, almost six, and the sun was setting. For this she was glad, because she had a feeling she was going to have to break in, and although the nearest neighbor lived probably a half-mile down the road and a line of trees hid the house from the road, she didn't want to be caught before she'd had a chance to plant her evidence. Just for kicks, she tried the front door. It was locked too. But she noticed the old wooden framed windows didn't lock. And in the back of the house there were screens missing. That gave her an idea.

She took the trash can out of the back seat, flipped it over and stood on it, then pushed up on the window. It slid up, not easily, but not as hard as she would've thought, considering the house had to be a hundred years old.

She climbed through, trying to be careful not to damage anything or leave traces of dirt on the floor or windowsill. Nervous, since she'd never broken into a house before, she worked quickly as she closed the window, went around to the back door, and opened it.

In three trips she had all the stuff unloaded from the car. She found an old wooden table in the basement, scattered the stuff about like she'd found it in Matt's house, found some newspapers upstairs and filled the trash can, then lit it on fire. After placing a call to 911 to report the fire, she ran out of the house and smack-dab into Jake's bulky body.

Immediately a few choice words rose up in her throat but before they found their way out of her mouth, Jake slapped his palm over her mouth and lifted a finger to his lips to hush her.

Murderer Numbers One and Two skulked past them toward the house as if they didn't even see her. The bottom half of her face still covered by Jake's hand, she twisted her neck to watch them. There were checking out Matt's car parked in the driveway.

"They can't see us but sometimes I think they hear us," Jake explained as he guided her toward the barn. "We can talk in here."

"Mhg-hmmm-mrmmm," she said, which was supposed to be, "You bet we will. I'd like to hear what you were doing in the truck with them if you weren't trying to help them." The second they stepped into the cool barn, she let it rip. "I saw you. What the heck were you doing in the truck with those creeps?"

"Helping you."

"Not helping them?"

"Why would I do that?" he asked, looking genuinely confused. "After all this time you don't trust me?"

"I've learned I'm not the best at weeding out the bad guys from the good guys these days. I was dead wrong about a guy I've known for years, literally. And since it looked like they were chatting with you like old friends, well, do you blame me for wondering?"

"No, not at all."

"So, you want to tell me how you ended up in their truck or are you going to leave me here hanging?"

"Wouldn't want to do that. I ran into the two gentlemen—and I use that term loosely—at the grocery store. Oh, hell!" He slapped his thigh. "I forgot about our steaks."

"That's okay. Just keep with the explanation. I'm eager to hear the rest." She sat on a hay bale and waited, wriggling a little bit at the itchy straw poking at her rear end through her jeans.

Standing, Jake bent his knee and set a foot next to her on the hay bale. "So, I was in the meat department picking out a couple of real nice New York strips for tonight and I heard those two yokels gabbing about a ghost swinging a lamp at them. I knew it was you." He chuckled. "Anyway,

I followed them out of the store and hitched a ride in their van. They didn't have a clue I was sitting right there. It was kind of fun. I messed with them a little bit."

"And?"

"They went to the office and talked to another guy. Ben."

"Ben was there?"

"Yep."

"Oh my gosh! And I just broke into his house thinking he was out of town. He could've caught me."

"Which leads me to my question: What the heck are you doing here?"

"I was just—" She cut off her sentence when she heard the howl of a siren. "Oh shoot! Matt's car!"

"Huh?"

"That's Matt's car out there in the driveway. It can't be there when the police arrive or all my plans will be ruined." She dashed out of the barn.

"Police?" he shouted, following her.

Shoving Murderer Number One aside, she opened the driver's side door and motioned for Jake to get into the passenger side. He moved quickly for a big guy, and within seconds the car was rolling over the grass, scaring the poop out of the two guys who had been moments earlier investigating it. They leaped out of the way just before she ran them over, not that she would've run them over on purpose. They deserved justice, but served by a Buick? She didn't have the stomach for that.

She turned onto the main road and drove in the opposite direction from which she'd originally come, hoping to avoid the police and fire trucks she could hear coming at full speed.

She saw the blinking red lights in her rearview mirror but forced herself to drive slowly to avoid calling attention to the car. She wasn't sure if the two men they'd left back at the farm would tell the police about the car or not, and she didn't know if the police officers could see her or not, and well, there were a lot of things she didn't know at the moment.

She drove several miles away and parked the car in a McDonald's parking lot. Finally fairly confident they weren't going to be pounced on by well-meaning public servants in blue, she turned to Jake. "Okay, so you were saying?"

"Huh?" he asked, his eyes wide, staring straight out the windshield, his arms braced against the dashboard. He looked like he'd just ridden with a first-day driver's ed student.

"You said the Murdering Twins talked to Ben. What did they say? What did Ben say? What did you say?"

"I didn't say anything. I just listened. But before I tell you about Ben and his sidekicks—reminds me of a song." He chuckled. "I want to know what that was all about up at the farm."

"I started a fire," she said flatly. "As they say, one act of unkindness deserves another."

"A fire?"

She nodded and opened the car door. "In fact, I'd like to take a walk, see if we can watch what's going on."

"Me too." He fell into step beside her as she hurried down the street.

"I took all that drug stuff they planted in Matt's house, plus Matt's laptop with the other evidence, and stuck it in Ben's basement. Then I lit a fire in the trash can and called the fire department and reported a fire."

"You . . ." He stopped walking and grabbed her shoulders. "You did what?"

She twisted her shoulders free and continued walking. "I don't want a lecture. Ben is a lowlife scumbag and he deserves what he's got coming, cute wife and dozen kids or not. He sent those killers to Matt's. We were friends. I held his newborn son, for God's sake. I . . ." Her nose burned and she knew tears were coming. Hot angry tears. "He killed me because he thought it would shut Matt up." The tears burst loose and ran down her cheeks. She didn't try to stop them, just wiped at them with her sleeve as she marched down the street. "That bastard had me killed for money."

"I'm so sorry, baby. I wish I'd been there when you found out." He wrapped a thick arm around her shoulders and pulled her to his side.

"It's okay." She shook her head and sniffled. "It was probably a good thing you weren't there. I wasn't exactly my best."

"But I don't care about that." He shook her shoulder. "Don't you realize that yet? Has all of this made you doubt me too?"

"Yes and no. I mean, you haven't done anything wrong. But gosh, one of my best friends was a cold-blooded murderer, and although my fiancé wasn't a killer he kept all kinds of secrets from me, things he should've told me. Those kinds of revelations shake a person's confidence in their ability to judge a person's character, you know."

"I understand." He sounded hurt and that hurt her, made her belly twist into an even tighter knot than it was already in.

"I'm sorry."

"No reason to apologize. You're being honest. I appreciate that." He let his arm fall off her shoulder but kept pace with her as she walked. "Your plan was ingenious, by the way."

"Thank you."

"Remind me to never get on your bad side."

She caught the teasing tone in his voice and smiled, despite the fact that her tears still hadn't dried completely. "You've been warned." She turned her head and looked up at him and he gave her a fleeting smile. She offered her hand and he took it.

His expression turned intense as he gave it a gentle

squeeze. "I hope someday I'll earn your unwavering trust."

"You deserve it. I'm just not sure if I'm ready to give it yet."

"I'm patient. I can wait."

They walked the rest of the way in silence. When they reached the Murdock's driveway, Claire hesitated. "Do you think it's wise to get any closer? What if someone sees us?"

"Claire, I don't think they can."

"Really? What makes you say that?"

"I did some experimenting while I was out this afternoon. I don't think any of the living can see us."

"But what about the waitress at Devil's Night and the people we helped that first day? And Barb at the office? What about Barb?"

"I can't explain those times, but I know there wasn't a soul who saw me in the grocery store." He led her down the driveway. "I jumped up and down and waved my arms in their faces. I blocked their paths. Not a single person looked me in the eye or spoke to me. If you think about it, outside of a person every now and then, no one has spoken to us."

Claire stopped walking and tried to replay in her mind the times she'd been in public. At the hospital, in the stores. Could she just have assumed they'd seen her? "Strange."

"Yeah. Strange. But here's the kicker: I think some of them can hear us." They stopped about twenty yards from the house and watched the police talking to the two murderers and the fire fighters putting away their equipment. Clearly, they were finished putting out the fire.

A rumble of car tires on dirt behind them sent them to the side of the driveway. Claire recognized Ben in the driver's seat as the car rolled by.

Ben parked the car and started talking to the police. He shook his head a lot. Two more police cars arrived. Later, as the moon crept high in the sky, casting a silver hue over the scene, the two murderers were handcuffed and put into one car and Ben was handcuffed and put into another. He did a lot of shouting at first, then seemed to accept what was happening. Willing to take a chance at being seen, Claire walked right up to the police car's rear window and glared at the bastard.

He looked back at her and visibly sucked in a breath. His eyes widened in shock. His pupils closed to the size of pin heads.

He saw her. No doubt about it.

She smiled and waved at him. When the officer got in the car and started it, she happily watched him being hauled away. "I hope you get the justice you deserve," she whispered.

"I have a feeling he will." Jake rubbed her arm. "It's late and I don't know about you but I haven't eaten in ages. Want to get something to eat before we . . . go back? Or is there something else you'd rather do?" he asked quietly.

"Something else. Definitely. Although I'm starving, I don't think I could eat right now. I think I need a little time to myself . . . for all this to sink in."

"I understand."

"Meet you back at the apartment in an hour?" she asked.

"Sure."

Claire frowned at the worry she heard in his voice and wished she could make things right with him the minute she returned. But if she was to have any hope of doing that, she first had some major soul-searching to do.

Chapter 20

After walking back to the car and driving around in circles for ten minutes or so, Claire found herself parked in Matt's driveway. She just sat in the car, staring straight ahead at his blinding-white garage door, lost in her thoughts.

Things had gone so differently from what she'd expected. Nine years of anticipating and planning had not prepared her for any of it.

One thing was clear: it was no wonder she'd met an early demise. She'd tripped along merrily through life, taking people and things at face value, never once suspecting they could be anything but what they appeared.

With her death and the subsequent reanimation came wisdom, but she had to be careful. Now that she knew the truth, and knew how easily she was fooled, she risked swinging in the opposite direction and trusting no one, including Jake.

As she'd walked and driven, she'd reminded herself that not every person who seemed great was a killer and not every friend an enemy in disguise, but in her heart she knew it would take more than a few minutes and an annoying chant to convince herself.

Time. It would take lots of time.

And that led her to her current dilemma. In the nine

days she'd spent with Jake he'd done nothing to earn her suspicion but be at the right place at the wrong time.

He'd given her support and guidance, love and reassurance, and now she was paying him back with fear and lack of faith. He deserved so much more.

She dropped her head back, closed her eyes, and sighed, but a light tap on the window didn't allow her to wallow in her worries. She rolled her head to the side and looked into Jake's concern-darkened eyes, then rolled down the window.

"I thought I'd find you here," he said.

"I had to return Matt's car."

"No, you needed to think up a good excuse to ditch me."

She held up a finger, indicating he needed to wait a minute, then hit the button on the automatic garage-door opener and parked the car. Still not sure what she would say to Jake when she stepped outside, she hit the button again to close the door and ran out before it hit the paved drive with a dull thump. "I swear, that's not what I was going to do," she said as soon as she was within earshot of him again.

"No?" His gaze traveled over her face, searched her eyes, bored deep into her soul.

She struggled to keep him out.

"I don't believe you. I see it. You've closed yourself off from me."

"Not intentionally," she denied.

"Yeah." His head dropped and he shook it slowly as his hands lifted and his fingers dragged through his dark curls, the light of the streetlamp shot silver blue highlights through them as they danced in an icy breeze.

"Jake, I'm sorry. I had no idea this would happen, that I'd learn my friends had betrayed me, that my fiancé had kept so many secrets. I'm trying to deal with this. Please. Please, try to understand. I don't want to hurt you." She started walking down the street, not really sure where she was headed. Back to the apartment, perhaps? Or just away, away from everyone and everything?

"If you tell me this is it, that we're through, you're going to hurt me," he said, falling into step beside her.

"You want me to feel guilty? I don't need this now."

"No. I don't want you to feel guilty." He caught her elbow and gave it a sharp tug, halting her. "But I want you to stop running."

"I'm not running. I'm walking. Let me go."

"Is that really what you want?"

"Yes . . ." She looked in his eyes and saw love and pain, joy and sorrow, hope and despair. She'd caused all those, good and bad. Could she stand the idea of hurting him more? "I don't know."

"Listen to me."

She nodded.

"Everything I told you was true. From my job as a doctor to the fact that I've been in love with you for almost fifteen years. I loved you so much I was willing to stand by and watch you marry another man. I loved you so much I was willing to search for you after I died and spend what little time I had here with you, doing whatever you wanted. I loved you enough to watch you struggle to find your answers without interfering when I was aching to keep you safe. Doesn't that say anything?"

"Yes," she whispered. It told her what she didn't want to hear: that she needed to love him with the same depth, to make the same sacrifices and accept the fact that loving him meant losing him, until she was able to trust again.

"Most of all, I love you enough to walk away right now, leaving my heart at your feet . . . because you're scared." He sighed and crossed his arms over his chest. "But I want you to answer one question before I go. Will you do that for me?"

She nodded.

"Do you love me too? Or am I just hoping for the impossible?"

She looked at his face, the face she'd come to adore, even as she faced her worst fears; the body that had given her pleasure as well as comfort; the spirit that had given her companionship as well as passion.

And she knew she had to tell him the truth. He deserved that much. "Yes. Very much."

"Okay. Thanks for telling me the truth." He blinked several times and turned away. His long legs carried him away from her quickly and she stood on the sidewalk, in the dark, watching his retreating back.

Her heart ached. A voice inside screamed for her to stop him before he was too far away. Another shouted to let him go, to spare him the pain of watching her struggle with her doubts, dragging him through the pain of proving himself worthy of her trust over and over again.

When he turned the corner, she dropped her face in her hands and swallowed back fierce tears. Tears of anger, of frustration and longing.

It wasn't fair to make him suffer like she knew he would. Everything she heard would be suspect for who knew how long. How could she be so cruel to ask him to live that way?

Still doubting the wisdom of her decision, she turned around and walked in the opposite direction. She walked past the apartment, then turned to say a final farewell to Devil's Night, a place she would never visit again.

Saturday night the place was packed. The deep bass of the music thrummed through the air as she stood under the streetlight and stared at the flickering neon sign in the grimy window. She saw the shadow of bodies moving about inside. The living. People with futures and families and friends.

She wondered how much longer she had until midnight. Maybe a half hour, maybe less. She silently waited, anxious to return to dull, gray purgatory. It was better than this place, where she was reminded of Jake, of what she could have had, of what was so cruelly stolen from her.

"You're letting them win," a voice beside her said. A child's voice.

She looked down. "Bonnie?"

"It's your afterlife, but I couldn't sit by and watch you do this without saying my piece. I've seen it all, I watched you pass, knew the answers you wanted to find."

"Why didn't you tell me? Why didn't someone tell me? I would've believed you."

"Because that's not the way it works. You had to find out for yourself."

"Well, I did. And look what it's cost me, and Jake. I hurt him, I know it. But he deserves someone who won't be questioning him all the time."

The little girl tossed a hand at her in dismissal. "Pish posh! That's just an excuse." She crossed her little arms over her chest and scowled.

"Is not." Having a three-year-old talking to her like this didn't sit well. How would a kid who died before kindergarten understand the intricacies of adult relationships? "No offense, but you wouldn't understand—"

"Like heck. I've been around a lot longer than you have, missy, despite my appearance. You need to learn to look beyond what you see."

"See? That's exactly my point. I don't know how."

"Follow your heart, listen to what your spirit tells you." The little girl gripped Claire's hands in her dainty little ones and squeezed. "Then you'll see people for whom and what they really are. You can do this. Just quit letting your fear of making a mistake stand in your way."

Claire nodded. "I always thought I could see past people's appearances. That's why I'm so unsure now."

The child shook her head. "You've only seen what your mind would let you see. Turn off the voices in your head.

Shut them up. They're obnoxious anyway. Trust your heart. Close your eyes," the child urged. "Close your eyes and trust your heart."

Claire closed her eyes and tried to see Bonnie for who she was: a wise person who was really not who she appeared, someone who she trusted and who annoyed her, someone who had guided her, always told her the truth, helped her. She blinked her eyes open, expecting to see an older woman, maybe her grandmother.

Jake smiled back at her. "You see now? How much I love you? You see me now."

"Yes," she whispered, shocked, confused. "You're Bonnie?"

He nodded.

"Then you tricked me."

"No, you tricked you. I've always been me. You saw what you expected to see."

"I expected to see a kid?" She stared down at the ground, tried to piece it all together. Bonnie was Jake. She . . . he . . . had helped and guided her right from the very start. He'd known what troubles she would face and had stood by, offering a helping hand when she asked for it, yet hadn't interfered when he would've liked to.

"Claire, I love you. I need to know, do you want to be together for always? Because if you do, you have to trust yourself and me. Do you?"

She knew the answer as she lifted her gaze and looked into his eyes. She saw the genuine love there and the sparkle of childlike hope. "Yes," she said. "I do."

"Then show me you trust me. Kiss me."

She tipped her head and pressed her lips to his. His smooth lips parted and his breath filled her mouth. She let her eyelids fall closed. She felt the world fall away and, fearful but grateful for his strength, she wrapped her arms around his neck and clung to him. Sounds dimmed, darkness faded to a dull gray, and the scents of Jake and crisp fall air slowly dissipated.

When she opened her eyes they were back in purgatory. She saw familiar faces: the man with the green toupee, the woman who had rolled her eyes when she'd sung the Madonna tune. "Hi. Funny seeing you here again."

They smiled but didn't speak.

"Do you know these people?" Jake asked.

"I saw them before I reanimated. The man was standing in front of me and this woman was in the line next to mine."

She looked at the man and woman again, then at Jake.

He shook his head. "Trust your heart. Look again."

Puzzled, she focused on the man and concentrated on feeling, not thinking. Before her eyes he changed shape, shifted, like the faces in that crazy Michael Jackson video. And then she saw who he really was—the waitress from Devil's Night, Janet, still wearing her little nurse's costume.

When she focused on the young woman, she changed to Barb.

They both smiled at Claire and for the first time in over a week, she knew she was seeing everyone as they really were.

And she knew another thing as well: she would never again look in the eye of the devil and see an angel.

"Thank you," she said to Jake, Barb, and Janet. "Thanks to all of you. I don't know how I'll ever repay you."

"You can't," teased Jake. "But I tell you one thing that could be a lot of fun." His eyes sparkled with mischief. "Let's meld. I've been waiting a long time to give it a try."

"Who am I to make you wait another minute, then?"

"Lie down and close your eyes," Jake whispered. The sound of his voice hummed through her spirit, buzzing and zapping like little charges of static electricity.

Alone with Jake, the others gone somewhere, she had no idea where, she lay in the cool gray nothingness and closed her eyes, shutting out everything but the sound of his voice and the soft caress of the gray mist as it whirled around her in little eddies.

"That's it. Now concentrate. Focus on my voice. Feel its warmth and energy."

Currents of heat washed through her soul as he spoke.

"Imagine we're still on earth, in bed. I'm touching you now. On your leg. Can you feel my soft caress?"

She felt it! A touch! To her shin. Soft and tickly, it traveled higher, over her knee to the crease between her upper thigh and her pelvis. "Yes. Yes, I do!" She shuddered.

"That's it. Now feel your heartbeat and breathing quicken as more heat pours through your body. My hand has traveled higher, over your stomach to your breast. My thumb is stroking your tight nipple. I want to suckle it. May I?"

She felt air filling her nonexistent lungs, felt blood pounding through a heart that didn't lie in her chest any longer. Felt liquid heat coursing through blood vessels that had long ago turned to dust.

His warm mouth found a nipple that couldn't be there, yet seemed to be.

She gasped. The sharp intake of air echoed through the bleak nothingness. She tried to open her eyes but felt his warm fingertips pressing on them.

"No, don't open your eyes. Once you see, it will end. Your faith isn't strong enough yet. Soon."

"Okay."

"Just focus on what you feel. What do you feel?"

She concentrated. The sensation of his tongue rasping over her sensitive nipple made her tremble. "I feel . . . I feel your tongue."

"Good."

Next, sharp teeth grazed her sensitive flesh, making her

moan, and fingers walking down her stomach made her muscles clench into a tight ball.

"That's it. Believe and it will be."

"Yes," she whispered. His fingertips felt warm on her flesh. His touch seared a path down the center of her stomach to her groin. When he parted her nether lips, she groaned and tossed her head from side to side. "Oh . . ."

"That's it. Believe."

Fingers slid up and down her slick flesh, slipping into her tight passage. Her inside muscles clenched around them and her legs trembled. Her heartbeat thudded in her ears. Loud and irregular and racing. Her heavy breathing echoed in the emptiness.

She felt him grip her thighs and slowly pulled them up and apart until she was open to him. Open and hungry for his intimate caress. The scent of her arousal teased her nostrils as his fingertips dug into the flesh of her thighs.

"I'm going to love you now." He rested his thick bulk over top of her.

"Yes. Oh yes." She wrapped her arms around his neck and gathered the silky curls at his nape in her fists. His erection slid along her slit, up and down, up and down, spreading the wetness of her need in his path.

Then it found her tight passage and slowly sunk inside.

She sighed, grateful for the fullness, and tipped her pelvis to take him deeper.

He drew out, then slowly slid back inside. "That's it, baby. I love you. So much. Take me," he whispered into her ear. Like his touches, the sound of his voice seemed to sink into her body, making her shudder. White hot sparks of pleasure zapped and sizzled between her thighs, sending waves of need into her stomach.

She slid her hands down over his shoulders, felt the flex of muscle under satiny skin as he moved. She lifted her head to kiss the skin, darted her tongue out to steal a salty sample.

His thick member plunged inside, in and out, in a steady rhythm. Overjoyed, she wrapped her legs around his narrow hips, taking him as deep as she could. Sensual friction on her sensitive nub spread a blanket of heat over her chest and face. Cool wetness coated her forehead, breasts, and stomach as her need grew and muscles tensed. She needed release. Every part of her body was coiled tight like an overwound spring. Muscles trembled and cramped. Blazes ignited throughout her body. Her mind floated in a haze of hot need.

"That's it. Take your release. I'm there."

Sparks flashed in the darkness as her gut clenched. Then a powerful orgasm surged through her body, making every muscle spasm and relax. Jake groaned in her ear, then slowed his pace. His intimate strokes made the pleasure of her release go on and on and on. She felt her soul twist and twirl through space with his, until they were one, literally, thinking the same thoughts, sharing the same sweet bliss. Then she felt them falling and pull apart.

Her heart full of joy, her mind lost in her pleasure and her body still tingling, she hugged him to her and sighed.

He stopped moving and rested on top of her a long while, then whispered, "Okay. Open your eyes."

When she lifted her eyelids, she saw they were still standing in the middle of the gray mist. She was wearing her nightie and cute feathered mules and he was wearing the jeans that hugged his butt and his smooth black leather jacket.

They weren't touching.

"Well?" he asked.

"Wow. I never would've thought it could be that great . . . without the parts or being able to touch, you know what I mean?"

"It's just as good, if not better, don't you think?"

"Yeah. Did I just imagine it or did we actually become one?"

"If you saw it with your heart, you know it's true. And we can do that whenever you like, for the next ten years. Until we can go down to Earth and do it again the regular way."

"If it's like that every time, who needs to go to Earth? I mean, Earth is great and all, but honestly, there's nothing for me there anymore."

Jake smiled. "That's what I've been waiting to hear for nine years."

Jake didn't actually hug her, but in her heart, Claire felt the warmth of his embrace and knew she'd found her love, her soul mate, the one who made her complete.

"Then again," she joked, "I'll miss those pink handcuffs."

"You don't have to miss them either," he said with a wicked grin. He spun around for a brief instant. When he turned to face her again, not one but two pairs were dangling from his index finger. "Like I said, if you can believe, then it will be."